D(

When Art and Magic Collide

Russell D. Bernstein

BRIGHTON PUBLISHING LLC
435 N. HARRIS DRIVE
MESA, AZ 85203

DOODLES
WHEN ART AND MAGIC COLLIDE

RUSSELL D. BERNSTEIN

BRIGHTON PUBLISHING LLC
435 N. HARRIS DRIVE
MESA, AZ 85203
WWW.BRIGHTONPUBLISHING.COM

ISBN13: 978-1-62183-218-8
ISBN 10: 1-621-83218-X

COPYRIGHT © 2014

PRINTED IN THE UNITED STATES OF AMERICA

First Edition

COVER DESIGN: TOM RODRIGUEZ

ALL RIGHTS RESERVED. THIS IS A WORK OF FICTION. ALL THE CHARACTERS IN THIS BOOK ARE FICTITIOUS AND THE CREATION OF THE AUTHOR'S IMAGINATION. ANY RESEMBLANCE TO OTHER CHARACTERS OR TO PERSONS LIVING OR DEAD IS PURELY COINCIDENTAL. NO PART OF THIS PUBLICATION MAY BE REPRODUCED OR TRANSMITTED IN ANY FORM OR BY ANY MEANS, ELECTRONIC OR MECHANICAL, INCLUDING PHOTOCOPY, RECORDING, OR ANY INFORMATION STORAGE RETRIEVAL SYSTEM, WITHOUT PERMISSION IN WRITING FROM THE COPYRIGHT OWNER.

Dedication

In loving memory of my mother, Billie; my aunt, Sherry; and my grandmother, Dinah. You were my inspiration, my anchors during storms, and always encouraged me to keep writing and dreaming. Above all else, you taught me to believe in myself. Your words of guidance showed me how powerful words can be. You are missed. You are loved.

Acknowledgements

This has been a long and difficult journey with unpredictable ups and downs, moments of wonder and excitement, and moments of apprehension and harsh reality. I could never have made it this far in the journey without my loving and supportive family and friends.

Special thanks to my beautiful wife, Holly, and my daughter, Brianne. You are my everything.

Helena Davison has guided me with her frankness with edits, invaluable direction—and most of all, her support from start-to-finish.

My father, Jeffrey; brother, Justin; and sister, Lindsay for inspiring me to read and to write even when I doubted myself.

To Reno Venturi and my fellow actors and writers at the Actor's Gym. Thank you for everything. Keep dreaming.

Thank you, Kathie McGuire, and the Brighton Publishing team for believing in me.

Without all of you, the pages would still be blank.

Review

The Sound Magazine

Connecticut Writer Crafts the Next Harry Potter?

Everyone knows the famous story of JK Rowling creating the billion-dollar *Harry Potter* franchise by allegedly handwriting the first book on the streets of England (or so the myth goes).

Well, it's possible the next *Harry Potter* was written last year by a Connecticut resident on his iPhone during what little spare time he had.

Russell D. Bernstein, who lives in Orange with his wife and daughter by way of Miami, spent the last few years crafting an imaginative adventure for kids, which combines the wizardly world of other successful children's novels with the inspiring and interactive world of art.

In *Doodles,* it's not just Wizardry, It's *WizARTry*!

Currently available at Amazon.com via Kindle and other electronic reading outlets, *Doodles* tells the story of a child who is given not just a magical wand, but a magical paint brush, which he can use to draw himself in or out of fantasies and predicaments. The brush proves to be a valuable tool in protecting the hidden world that needs his help.

Harry Potter and other fantasy books open the mind of a child, but a story like *Doodles* also directs them towards a particular way of expressing themselves. In this case, it's painting, drawing, or art in general. Why just pick up your magic wand and imagine a dragon appearing when that same child can draw that dragon, taking it right from his imagination onto a piece of paper, actually making it appear in reality? By turning a paintbrush into a wand, Bernstein is encouraging children to actually create the fantasies they imagine.

Bernstein has already finished the first draft of the *Doodles* sequel and hopes that the series can become a fantasy mainstay for the digital age we live in today. With bullying extremely prevalent in schools today, stories like *Doodles* have become more and more important in guiding youngsters through tough times in and outside the classroom.

~ Scott Yager – Managing Editor

Chapter One

THE HIDDEN MESSAGE

"The most beautiful thing we can experience is the mysterious.
It is the source of all true art and science."
~ Albert Einstein

"**G**et him!"
"Don't let him get away!"

Three kids ran down an alleyway, yelling and screaming taunts at a boy who was clearly running out of energy. He was flailing his arms and moving his legs as fast as they would carry him.

"You can't run forever, Loser!"

"Yeah, quit making us...run so much." One of the chasers was unmistakably heavier than the others and was

1

winded. "When we…get a hold…of you Doodles, you're toast!"

Doodles ran, and when he felt like he couldn't run anymore, he ran even harder. He was used to this—eventually they would give up and go away. At least, that was what normally happened. It was almost as if this was some sort of cruel cat and mouse game and, unfortunately, he was the mouse.

This was his neighborhood, though, and as he got closer to his house, he led the kids down alleyways and even in circles at some points. He knew every street and hiding place by heart. There'd been many times when this knowledge had come in handy.

Doodles tried to keep his mind off of the danger he was in. If he thought about other things, it helped him cope with difficult situations like this one.

Just as Doodles was about to duck into his favorite hiding place—a tight space between two dumpsters—a hand grabbed his shoulder and turned him around.

"Where ya going?" It was the tallest of the pursuers and the smirk on his face made Doodles nearly scream. "You think you can get away from us?"

"Just let me go!" Doodles shouted as he tried to squirm out of his grip.

"Or what? You can't draw yourself out of this one," the kid smirked as he pulled Doodles even closer. "Tell you what I am gonna do. I'll let you go without throwing you into the dumpster if you give me five dollars. Sounds more than fair, doesn't it?"

Doodles gulped. He believed the kid. The only problem was that he didn't have any money on him.

He suddenly stepped down as hard as he could manage on the bully's toes. As the kid screamed out in pain, he loosened his grip for just a second, allowing Doodles to run on.

"I'll get you for that Doodles! Wait until Monday!" the bully yelled as he hopped up and down in pain. His voice trailed off as Doodles ran away.

He'd never run so fast in his life. As he got to his house, he decided to go in through his bedroom window to avoid being questioned by his parents. This was easier said than done as his room was on the second floor. Doodles reached up and grabbed the branch of a tree. Hoisting himself up, he regained his balance before proceeding across the narrow branch to his window. When he finally made his way to the window, he promptly fell through the opening, onto the floor, legs and arms sprawled out in all directions.

Sadly, it was a typical day in the life of Doodles Lanhorn.

Doodles wasn't the sort of kid who laughed at others or called them silly names or did anything that was considered mean. He was a loner, a kid who kept to himself and didn't interfere in the lives of others. It wasn't like he didn't have any friends or family, though. His mom and dad adored him, proudly proclaiming to the whole neighborhood that their son was an angel. Doodles' aunt and uncle lived just two blocks away, and reminded him daily that he had a huge heart. Doodles didn't mind the attention and praise when he was younger, but he sure didn't enjoy it anymore. He was twelve now and felt like something was missing from his life. He had a loving family, lived in a nice house, and was generally healthy, but he felt empty inside. The kind of empty you get if you are by yourself in a dark movie theater. No, it was deeper than that— more like knowing you were meant for something greater, and never finding out what that was.

Doodles wasn't ugly by any means, but he wasn't exactly handsome either. His red hair was unruly and constantly fell over his eyes. He was tall for his age, so he at least had that going for him. Unfortunately, this also made him lanky and awkward when he walked, and set him up to fail miserably at any sport. He, however, wasn't interested in sports no matter how much his family tried to get him to play. His dad was by far the worst, always asking Doodles to come outside to play this or that. Sometimes he humored his father, if only because he didn't want to let him down. But this night, with his birthday coming soon, he only wanted to be by himself. Doodles' room was his sanctuary to draw and think about his life.

The last week had been especially tough on Doodles. On Friday, he had sat in the back of the room in his usual seat during study hall. Every other kid was busy talking to their friends as the teacher read a magazine. She barely noticed the kids at all since she was so engrossed in Fashion Weekly.

Doodles couldn't understand how these kids made friends so easily. The few friendships he had weren't easy to make. Doodles usually passed study hall by actually studying— a novelty the other kids were apparently unaware of—or by daydreaming and sketching. During this study hall session, Doodles spent the entire time sketching in the air. It was amazing how he could almost see traces of light where he moved his hands. Sometimes the tracings of light would remain for several seconds. Doodles tried to hide this behind his class books for fear of being called a freak, and he certainly didn't share this with his parents. He knew this wasn't normal, but didn't really understand it enough himself to share it with anyone.

When the bell rang, Doodles gathered his books and went to put them in his locker. When he got there, however, he quickly noticed that sticky gum had been smeared all over it.

Someone had gone to great lengths to place the gum squarely on the locker's handle, right where he'd have to put his hand onto it to open it.

Doodles grabbed some paper towels from the bathroom and used them to open the locker door. He sighed.

Doodles was torn away from his thoughts of the school week by a chill coming in from the open window. He got up and closed it. Despite the cold, Doodles was usually warmed by the escape from reality drawing provided him. He didn't have to think about the bullies at school or humoring his father by pretending to enjoy sports, or whatever else his boring life asked of him. This was his time. He could draw whatever he imagined. Unlike real life, he could control the outcome. And so it came to be that this night—the third of December—a twelve-year-old boy named Doodles Lanhorn fell asleep with a pencil still in hand.

His dreams were filled with images of his drawings come to life. His dreams were so real, so vivid, that he could usually remember every detail and color upon awakening.

Hours passed until Doodles awoke with a start, realizing that he had fallen asleep on the floor again.

"Doodles, are you coming to breakfast?" His mom's voice carried across the entire house; it always seemed to find him no matter where he was.

He didn't bother responding. He knew that his mother only called once, and it was first come first served on Pancake Saturdays. He would've kept laying there for a bit, trying to catch a little more sleep, but he remembered that his mom had invited his uncle and aunt over for breakfast this particular Saturday. With anyone else that wouldn't matter so much, but his Uncle Roger was almost three hundred pounds. Last summer, he had won the town's pie eating contest, and by all accounts, it wasn't even a close race. Doodles was in such a hurry that he completely forgot that he was in his rumpled clothes from the day before.

"Doodles! Uncle Roger has already had two servings!" his dad warned from downstairs.

Doodles pushed open his door and slid down the stairway banister with rehearsed ease. Well, almost, save for bumping his elbow on the end. He ignored the pain as he hurried into the kitchen. It was Pancake Saturday after all.

Just as he was about to join the rest at the table his mother appeared with a disapproving scowl on her face.

"Are those the clothes you slept in last night."

It wasn't a question. It was a statement that clearly meant no food before changing clothes. She reminded Doodles of one of those large Egyptian statues that guarded the ancient pyramids. He looked at the serving plate of pancakes and realized that in another few minutes there might not be any more.

Suddenly Uncle Roger gave out a huge, bellowing laugh, his great stomach puffing out like a water balloon about to burst. With a friendly smile he said, "Oh, come now. Let the boy eat, Emily. He's a growing boy after all. There's no sense in him changing on account of us. You were always a tough one growing up." He waved a finger at her mockingly.

Doodles looked at his uncle thankfully and then back to his mother pleadingly.

Emily held her scowl for a moment longer, sighed in resignation, and rolled her eyes with exaggeration.

"Very well, but just this once," Mrs. Lanhorn said as she began to wash dishes. She straightened out her apron and brushed back her long, red hair. Doodles sat down as his uncle winked at him cheerfully. Uncle Roger hummed while stuffing more pancakes into his mouth, his rosy cheeks puffing outward in satisfaction. His dark blue eyes lit up in anticipation as his wife passed another plate of pancakes his way. Uncle Roger patted his wife on the shoulder and they shared a loving look for a moment.

His Aunt Martha wiped some syrup off of her husband's chin and folded the napkin back up neatly. She was a woman who was always well-dressed regardless of the occasion, and believed in proper manners at all times. Her posture would make a drill sergeant jealous, and her long, brown hair was always pulled into a perfectly neat bun. She was the complete opposite of her slovenly husband.

"Doodles, mind your manners," she said after she cleared her throat.

Doodles paused long enough to say, "Sorry. Hi Aunt Martha," before stuffing a chocolate chip pancake into his mouth.

Uncle Roger smiled. "Heavens, looks like the boy hasn't eaten in days."

In response, Doodles slowed down and let his long hair fall over his eyes to hide his embarrassment.

His mother pointedly cleared her throat as well. "And someone's birthday is coming up soon…"

Doodles looked up between mouthfuls. "Don't remind me."

Aunt Martha smiled knowingly. "Well we didn't need to be reminded. I know your birthday isn't until Monday, but we simply couldn't wait to give you your gift. After all of your hard work at school you deserve it."

Doodles mumbled a thank you as his dad clapped him on the back. Then, Mr. Lanhorn's dark, black eyes narrowed as he leaned forward. He was one of the town's toughest lawyers, and in this moment, Doodles knew why people called him "Bill the Unforgiving." Well, not to his face, anyway.

"And maybe next year Doodles will try out for basketball. With his height—"

His mother gave a look that cut Bill off instantly. Doodles always thought it was amusing that a tiny woman like his mother could bring Bill the Unforgiving to silence. If only his opponents in court could see him now.

"Well, we will talk about that another time," his father continued. "Either way, we are all proud of you." His father wasn't a mean man. He was just tough sometimes. His nickname came from his work. At home he was a stern, yet fair, father.

Doodles managed his best, practiced smile, and although he knew he should be happy, he just couldn't help but think that there was something missing...something important that just wasn't there in his life.

Doodles wasn't sure how he found himself squished between his uncle and aunt on the living room couch. All he knew was that this particular couch was clearly not meant to fit the three of them. He remembered being quickly ushered from the kitchen table by his aunt and uncle, followed excitedly by his mother and father.

"Well, here you go," Uncle Roger said cheerfully while his rosy cheeks almost made Doodles give a genuine smile. Almost. He handed a carefully wrapped gift to Doodles who managed to squirm his arms free.

"We know you'll like it," his uncle added gleefully.

Doodles opened it carefully, half-expecting a prank of some kind. This was the same uncle who only last Christmas decided it would be hilarious to fill his stockings with chocolate pudding. Doodles remembered vividly reaching his hands into warm, gooey…

"Doodles. Open it already," his father said.

He realized he had paused for quite some time now and finished opening the gift. It was a book—a large book. He hid his disappointment. He didn't really like to read.

"Thank you," he said. When they didn't respond he added, "It's nice."

His aunt and uncle looked at each other and smiled. "Well, aren't you going to open it up?" His aunt and uncle were clearly very excited as they leaned in closer to Doodles, squeezing him even more.

He opened the book, surprising him by how nice the leather felt on the outside. The pages were filled with fantastic drawings. He couldn't hide his surprise and excitement. They were beautiful—clearly done by a master of the craft. Doodles marveled at the intricate detail and time that must have gone in to something like this. Each page was better than the last. He held the book close to his chest.

"It's—it's beautiful," he said at last as he gave a genuine smile.

Doodles couldn't wait to take the book up to his room to examine it more closely. From a quick glance, it looked like there were different drawings in this book, each equally as beautiful and intricate. He excused himself, quickly thanking his aunt and uncle, as he ran up the stairs to his bedroom three stairs at a time.

The book was truly a work of art. He'd never seen something so grand. The leather was dark amber with golden borders. The border patterns were loopy waves, rising and falling with majestic precision. The waves crashed in the middle to form the title in the center of the cover. The lettering of the title had been created with a fine, gold filigree, and it was inlaid with a ruby in the center. It was a thick book, heavier than any book he had ever held. The title *Wizartry* made the hair on the back of his neck stand on end. Something about the title made his pulse quicken. He turned to the first page.

The first drawing was of a magical city in the clouds. There were all sorts of strange and fanciful buildings. Each of the buildings represented different aspects of nature.

Another page was of a giant river running through a forest filled with purple trees. The trees were teeming with beautiful creatures, some of them bird-like, while others bore resemblances to monkeys, swinging from tree to tree with long arms. Even more impressive was a bronze dragon guarding a hoard of treasure, her wings curled around the mounds of gold, coins, and jewels like a protective mother.

There were also descriptions on each page, written in loopy gold letters. The drawings needed no descriptions, though. They set Doodles' imagination on fire. As he reached the last page, he stopped abruptly and squinted. This writing had clearly been done in a different pen, written in tiny blue letters. It was difficult to make out. He had to bring his face within an inch of the writing to make it out.

He read out loud, "To learn real magic, come to the bookstore on Lamter Lane. Knock three times and only three." Doodles read it again just to be certain. That was silly. Perhaps the author owned the bookstore and wanted more business. But that made no sense because bookstores have nothing to do with magic. And magic—well that was just sleight of hand and well-practiced tricks. Then, what did the message in the book mean?

Lamter Lane was only a few miles from home. Strange that it should be so close. Perhaps that is where his aunt and uncle had bought the book. Doodles wasn't positive that he remembered a bookstore there, but he couldn't be sure. Tomorrow he could ride his bike there. If nothing else, he could put his curiosity to rest.

Little did Doodles know that the words on the last page would change his life—forever.

Chapter Two

RIDDLEY

It wasn't going to be easy to convince his parents to let him go for a bike ride. It was raining, after all, and he sure wasn't going to ask either of them for a ride in their station wagon. They would ask him tons of questions like they always did, and Doodles didn't feel like explaining what he was up to. Actually, come to think of it, Doodles didn't really know what he was up to either.

"Dad, I'm twelve now-almost thirteen. I'm just going for a bike ride," Doodles protested.

His father looked up from his morning newspaper and gave Doodles an all-too-familiar stern look. Shaking his head, Mr. Lanhorn said, "I gave my answer." He went back to reading.

Mrs. Lanhorn overheard them talking and entered the living room. "Your father has a point, Doodles. It is raining outside." She handed Bill a glass of water with three ice cubes, just like always.

"What if I promise to go to church next weekend and I won't complain at all about having to dress up?" Doodles was desperate now. His curiosity of the message in the book was overwhelming.

"Now you are talking like a real negotiator. Make it three weekends in a row, and then try out for the basketball team, and you have a deal, mister," his father said.

Doodles was about to respond when his mother chimed in. "Honey, it's raining outside."

"It will build character," Bill said, waving his hands dismissively. "Well Doodles, what do you say? Three weeks of church in a row and no complaining."

Doodles tried to hide his smile. "Deal."

Before his parents could say anything else, he was off, pedaling as fast as his legs would take him. It had been a long time since he rode a bike and it took most of his energy to keep it from swerving all over the road. The rain sure didn't help either. It made it extremely difficult to hold on to the grips, especially when going over bumps or through puddles. Doodles found that he didn't mind the rain so much after a while. It felt nice on his face and he had to admit that he felt a bit rebellious riding in the rain.

Two miles went by faster than he thought. Lamter Lane was a small road near Dockside, a part of town that was known for its seafood and carnivals. Lamter Lane was about a half-mile long with brick stores packed tightly together. Today they gave the impression of being huddled together for warmth against the rain. Doodles thought that maybe he'd been here once but he couldn't remember.

There were only a handful of people out and most were hurrying to wherever their destinations were. The rain was coming down harder now. It was beginning to hail and felt like tiny needles stinging his entire body all at once. Doodles sped up and scanned the signs of the shops, looking for the one he wanted.

Just as he was about to put his search on hold and duck into any shop to avoid the rain, he spotted what he was looking for. There was nothing special about it—red brick, small white sign, plain door. If Doodles hadn't been looking for something he would have never seen it. The building was nondescript except for a small sign on the side of the front wall. The sign read *Magic Bookstore*. This had to be it. Doodles hopped off of his bike, nearly tripping over his own feet, and then leaned the bike against the front wall. He was about to run inside when he remembered the message in the book. It seemed silly to follow the directions, especially in the rain, but even so he found himself knocking three times and then waiting. It felt like ages passed before the door finally swung open. What Doodles saw wasn't at all what he expected.

The door seemed to have opened by itself. Doodles would have spent some time trying to find out how a wooden door would be able to do something like that, but he was too distracted by what he saw inside. Or more correctly, what he didn't see.

The room was deceptively large, its wooden floorboards stretching in all directions. It almost seemed impossibly vast, and if Doodles wasn't further distracted by what was in the middle of the room, he would have gone back outside to compare the relative size of the small outer wall.

In the middle of the room was a solitary, simple wooden chair. On the chair sat an unimpressive, old man with a long white mustache and a dark black hat with a yellow brim. He reminded Doodles of an old sea captain he once met when his family went on a boat ride in Dockside. Only this man was skinny—almost too skinny—with his collarbones clearly standing out through his far-too-tight T-shirt. His skin was far too pale to be a sea captain, and his almond-shaped eyes made him look like he was from some other continent. Doodles would guess he was from Asia, but the pale skin threw him off from pinpointing. The man was looking at him, and Doodles felt the need to say something—anything—to break the awkward silence that was there except for the pitter patter of the rain outside.

"This can't be right..." He looked around as if expecting to find something else to prove he was in the bookstore.

"What can't be right?" the old man asked, his voice sounding dull and deep in the silent room.

"I thought this was a bookstore." Doodles looked down at his shoes and realized ashamedly that he had dragged in quite a bit of mud.

Seeming to read his thoughts, the man laughed gently. "Don't worry about the mud. I'll clean it up later."

"Are you renovating? Where are all the books? Where are all the magic tricks?"

At this, the man stopped smiling. "Did you say magic tricks?"

Doodles looked uncertain and glanced back at the door nervously. "Well, yes. I read about it in a book."

"Ah. Well, that makes more sense now, doesn't it? I mean, who knocks three times in the rain and then just stands there in front of an obviously open shop? I should have figured you were here for that."

"For what, sir?"

The man leaned forward, his dark grey eyes scanning Doodles as if judging him. "For magic, of course."

"But there isn't anything here."

Just as Doodles said this the old man leaned slightly to the right and Doodles caught a glimpse of an artist's easel that he could have sworn wasn't there before.

The man laughed again and stood up on shaky legs. He steadied himself with the arm of the chair and then stepped sideways to reveal a good view of the easel fit with buckets of paint, paper, and a long brush. With an exaggerated flourish he swept his arms outward and pointed to the easel. "Everything you could ever want, dream about, or read about is here, my dear boy."

"What do you mean 'everything'?" Doodles' eyebrows rose quizzically. He no longer cared about the rain or how it was almost Monday and that meant school tomorrow. All of his curiosity was focused on this strange man and his easel.

"What is your name, boy?" The old man attempted to smile, but his teeth were crooked and his lips curled at the end, coming across to Doodles as somewhat mischievous.

He thought of giving a fake name, but something compelled him to be honest with this man. His eyes were so honest and inviting. "Doodles. My name is Doodles."

"Ah. A very fitting name for a Wizart."

"I don't know what a Wizart is, and I don't know the first thing about magic, sir. And to be honest, I'm not really into all of that stuff. I don't mean to be disrespectful…" Doodles trailed off with a shrug. He followed up with a smile when he realized he might have offended the old man.

The man frowned slightly at the comment and then sighed, his breath rattling around inside his throat. "You don't believe in magic? Why are you here then?"

Doodles looked down at his shoes and shrugged. "I guess I was curious, sir."

"Do me a favor?" the old man asked. "Call me Riddley. It's my name after all. And if I'm to be training you, I'd expect you to at least know my name."

Doodles looked him over and almost laughed. "Train me? Didn't you hear me, Riddley? I said I'm not interested in magic. Is this some kind of joke?"

Riddley ignored the question, bent down, and then picked up the dripping paintbrush. Despite his age, he was surprisingly quick, and before Doodles knew it, Riddley was standing right in front of him, paintbrush in hand. "Take it."

Doodles looked at the paintbrush suspiciously and then back to the old man. "I'm sorry?"

"Take it and show me what you know so far." His voice was calm and authoritative.

Doodles wanted to ask more questions, but the man was standing there waiting. The whole situation was odd. Normally, Doodles would have run off, but he found himself full of curiosity. For some reason, he felt compelled to grab the brush and paint. And so he did.

At first, he was nervous and felt awkward, but then it seemed to come naturally to him. He remembered the beautiful drawings in the book and tried his best to reproduce one of them. He chose one of the easier paintings, not that any of them were easy by any means. He dipped the paintbrush into one of the cans of paint labeled Gold, and then brought it up to the canvas. His hand moved with ease, as drawing was his passion. Familiarity set in. When Doodles was finished, he looked up and waited.

The old man named Riddley smiled appreciatively. "Now, we do magic."

Doodles was markedly impressed by what he had painted. It wasn't quite as good as the book his uncle and aunt gave him, but it was certainly one of the best paintings *he* had ever created. It was of a golden sword with a jewel-encrusted leather handle. The blade itself glowed with an unearthly brightness that seemed to illuminate the room Doodles stood in.

"Now, we add this. The secret ingredient," Riddley said from behind Doodles.

He nearly jumped out of his shoes in surprise. He was so enthralled by what he had drawn that he hadn't noticed Riddley approach from behind him.

Riddley held up a small, black vial filled with dark black paint. He sniffed it, causing his mustache to wiggle comically up and down. He swirled it around a few times and then held it out toward Doodles.

"Why would we cover it in black? Won't that just mess everything up?" Doodles tried to act casual, but the whole situation was unnerving, and his voice was shaky at best.

Riddley laughed. It sounded like two iron grates grinding against each other. It made Doodles' skin crawl. "You can't complete the spell without the final touch. Any respectable Wizart knows that," Riddley stated as if it were the most obvious thing in the world.

Doodles shrugged. After what he had already heard today, this was not the weirdest comment so far. He didn't want to mess up his drawing, but he also wanted to find out what this old man was talking about. In the end, curiosity won over.

"How much does it need?" Doodles inquired.

Riddley looked around the room as if lost in thought. "Huh? How much does what need?"

Doodles resisted the urge to roll his eyes. "The painting. How much of the special ingredient does it need?"

Riddley thought for a moment, opened his mouth to speak, closed it, and then spoke, his tone serious, "Only as much as is required. Too much and you will not be able to control it. Too little and it might come out with two heads and a mustache."

Doodles didn't really quite understand what Riddley was getting at, and quite frankly he was beginning to think the old man was crazy. But he had come this far, so he might as well humor the man, just as he did when his dad asked him to play basketball or some other sport.

Doodles applied the paint, slowly at first, occasionally glancing back toward Riddley to gauge his expression. It was blank however, and this was of no help to Doodles. The paint now covered the entire sword he'd created. With one last sweep of the brush, he finished, and then stepped back.

At first, nothing happened. Doodles started to become upset that he had just ruined a perfectly good painting. He was about to say so when suddenly there was a popping noise, like the sound a sputtering engine makes when it struggles to start. The sound persisted for a good twenty or so seconds and then Pop! The page went blank.

Doodles turned to the old man in disbelief. "What happened? Where is it?"

Riddley pointed, his bony finger extending toward the floor. "See for yourself."

There, on the wooden floor, was the exact sword he had painted. Only it wasn't a painting…*it was real.*

Doodles bent down and picked up the sword, feeling the warm, leather handle and how heavy it felt in his hands. "This—this can't be real."

"It can't?" Riddley asked with amusement. "Then explain to me what you're holding."

Doodles couldn't come up with a reply. He was dumfounded. The sword felt as solid as anything he'd ever held. It was a surreal feeling, almost as if he were in a dream—except this wasn't a dream.

Riddley continued. "Well, you can't just leave it here. Off with you then. I will see you tomorrow afternoon for your next lesson." He started to shoo Doodles toward the door.

"Wait, what? I have school tomorrow." Doodles tried to slow down, but Riddley's shoving proved to be surprisingly strong.

"After school then. Go on. Plenty of customers I have to worry about." Riddley gave him a final shove, and before Doodles knew what had happened, he was outside and the door closed behind him.

He stood there, sword in hand, and his mouth open in shock. What an odd man. At least it had stopped raining. He wondered how long he had been inside. Looking around he spotted a dumpster. He obviously couldn't take the sword home. What would his parents say? He gave one last longing look as it would be rather neat to keep it, and then tossed it into the dumpster.

When he looked around for his bike, he saw three kids standing by it.

"I thought I recognized your old bike, Doodles. What are you doing on this side of town anyways?" the largest of the three spoke.

Doodles recognized him. It was Brandon. He was one of the older kids in the school and known for his dislike of younger kids. He was a good head taller than Doodles and his arms were twice as muscular. The other two snickered at Brandon's comment and knocked over Doodles' bike.

"Leave me alone, Brandon," Doodles said before he could think better of it. He tried to sound more confident than he felt, but his voice wound up cracking.

"Or what? Are you going to draw a picture of me? You're a loser, Doodles, and you always will be," Brandon said as he kicked the bike.

Again the other two laughed.

"Come on guys, I don't want to waste any more of my time with this loser."

They started to head off and then Brandon turned back around, saying "Hey Doodles, let me know when you draw yourself a friend."

Doodles now wished that it had still been raining because it would have hid his tears.

He decided to walk home instead of riding. He strolled slowly, holding onto his bike. He was full of conflicting emotions. He was angry at those idiots outside of the bookstore, and he was confused and excited all at once about what happened with the sword, and he was suspicious of the old man's intentions.

He didn't realize how tired he was until he got home. Today had been more than eventful, and so when he entered the house, he slumped down on the couch with a big sigh. His shoulders felt like he had been carrying lead weights all day, and his arms were hurting from gripping the bike so tightly.

His father looked up from his newspaper. "You do know your mother will kill you if she sees you sitting there in those damp clothes." He gave Doodles an expectant look and went back to reading his newspaper.

Doodles almost wanted to chance it, but then he remembered times in the past that what he had thought was a good idea at the time always led to him being grounded. He decided it was best to change out of his damp, muddy clothes and not to tempt fate. It took him a while to clean up and change, as he was still lost in deep thought about the day's happenings. On his way down the stairs, he heard his aunt and uncle's voices. What he overheard made him stop mid-step.

"He did well today." It was his uncle's voice. "Got a good review and he never gives out good reviews on the first day."

Doodles tried to sneak closer, but the voices carried off as they must have gone outside. He wanted to run downstairs and hear more before his aunt and uncle left. Instead, he crept downstairs and took his place on his favorite couch in the living room. It was one of those couches that looked ridiculously comfortable and felt even more so in reality. He picked up a magazine and pretended to read so that his parents would leave him alone. He needed something to keep him distracted. Thinking about the day's events was making his head spin.

Should he go to the bookstore after school tomorrow? What would he tell his parents? What if he had imagined all of it? Doodles didn't really remember the rest of the night. His body went through the motions, but his mind was elsewhere.

Chapter Three

SCHOOL

School was boring. Doodles tried at first to keep his mind off of the magic bookstore by concentrating really hard on his teachers and their desperate attempts to earn the attention of thirty rowdy students. When that didn't work, he began to draw. He almost succeeded until he thought about how neat it would be to have some of that special ingredient Riddley showed him to make his drawings come to life.

It took three whole classes before Doodles realized he couldn't ignore the fact that he was curious, and the only way to ease his curiosity would be to return to the bookstore. His mind set, the day went by much easier. It was like he was giving up fighting against an impossibly giant wave of curiosity and simply riding it wherever it took him.

During fifth period, however, things started to go downhill. Doodles took his usual seat in the back row. Mr. Thompson was quite possibly the most boring teacher he had ever had the displeasure of having. It wasn't only because the subject itself was dull. He had a voice that was completely monotone—and it really didn't help that the subject was algebra.

This was the one class Doodles had trouble in. It wasn't for lack of effort. Mr. Thompson's notorious lectures simply made Doodles daydream.

Doodles started to trace in the air with his hand, making outlines of anything that came to mind. Sometimes he could see traces of light where he had just moved his hand. He noticed a kid staring at him and snickering so he started to scribble drawings on his notepad instead. Doodles was in the middle of sketching a motorcycle he had seen once at a fair when Mr. Thompson cleared his throat loudly.

"Mr. Lanhorn. I am assuming that since you are drawing, you've already mastered Algebra, and that it is now beneath you."

Before Doodles could reply, Mr. Thompson continued, "Class, you can all thank Mr. Lanhorn for the pop quiz today. Clear your desks."

The class moaned and Doodles slunk down as far as he could in his seat.

Thankfully, lunchtime came quickly. The cafeteria was huge considering that there were not nearly as many kids in his school as the schools in neighboring towns. There were many circular wooden tables spread out in no apparent order.

Doodles sat at his usual table with all of the other "misfits" as he liked to call them. There was Jimmy—he was quite possibly the smallest kid in the entire school. His ears stuck out to the side, and most of the other kids called him Elf. There was Darren—he was normal looking until he opened his mouth. Once he started talking, the kid wouldn't stop. He made Doodles' social skills look great by comparison.

And then there was Laura. She was beautiful in Doodles' mind. She had this carefree attitude about life in general that he admired and found appealing. She was also a big fan of his artwork, always asking him to draw vampires and other dark creatures. Laura loved artwork, and Doodles could never refuse her request for a drawing. She had long, black hair that curled up at the ends. She was a tomboy and didn't really fit in to the other cliques at school. Doodles thought she was perfect, though. Sometimes he found himself staring at her.

It was exactly one of these moments that Laura looked up and Doodles awkwardly shifted his attention to playing with his mashed potatoes. She laughed and Doodles tried to hide his embarrassment. Their lunch was the usual on Tuesdays-hamburgers and mashed potatoes, and something the school passed off as a vegetable. It was more like a bunch of vegetables mashed together.

Darren, not surprisingly, spoke first, "There's a new kid in school. His name is Scott. I'm thinking about inviting him to our table one day. What do you guys think?" He didn't wait for an answer, "Yeah, I'll invite him. He seems nice."

Laura smiled. "Happy birthday Doodles. You look distracted today." Her voice was soft and beautiful, and in that moment, he almost forgot all of his worries.

Doodles wanted to share with them his news, but how could he? He didn't really understand it himself. Maybe when he learned more he would share it with them. "I'm just tired, that's all."

Darren spoke up again, "Stayed up late drawing again?" He answered his own question before Doodles could, "Of course you did. Draw anything good? Yes? I wish I could draw like you."

The bell rang, signaling the end of lunch. Doodles was thankful for the interruption. The end of the school day was coming up fast and he was getting more and more excited for things to come.

For Doodles, the last period of the day was gym class. This worked out well because if it had been earlier in the day, he would have to go about the rest of the day all sweaty. Most kids probably didn't mind, but he was self-conscious about those kinds of things. He definitely wouldn't be able to sit next to Laura if he was all sweaty.

Today was basketball. His dad would be happy about that. The other kids usually laughed at the way he dribbled the ball. Doodles didn't really care today. He was so excited about returning to the bookstore that he happily waited to be picked last for teams.

"Doodles, pay attention!"

The basketball bounced right in front of him three times as his teammate called out. Doodles watched as the ball went out of bounds.

"Seriously? At least pretend to try," the kid said as he went to retrieve the ball. He gave Doodles a shove as he went by. Doodles looked up to see the gym teacher looking their way. He thought the teacher might actually intervene this time, but Mr. Garrett shrugged and went back to the book he was reading.

Doodles didn't care whether the kid thought he was trying or not. Kids were mean even if he did try. The only kids in the whole school that even cared about him were Laura, Darren, and Jimmy.

His parents knew that he was picked on sometimes, but he never shared with them how bad it really was. Maybe things were different at other schools. The teachers here didn't really seem to try to prevent it. He didn't understand why people acted mean. Doodles never bullied anyone.

Before long, gym would be over and he wouldn't have to worry about these other kids. The bookstore and its mysteries awaited him.

Doodles knocked three times and waited. Just like last time, it took a good minute before the door swung open of its own accord.

"You're late," Riddley admonished, sitting on the only chair in the entire room. He tapped his foot impatiently on the floorboards.

"Late? I didn't know we made an exact time to—" Doodles said as he nearly forgot to close the door.

"I assume you studied for your first test?" Riddley cut him off mid-sentence.

He was confused. The old man had a way of keeping Doodles off-balance and it was starting to irritate him.

"Test?" Doodles closed the door far harder than was necessary. He normally didn't let his anger get the best of him but he was completely flustered at this point.

Riddley gave a big sigh, letting his breath slowly leak out of him. "I swear that sometimes I think you don't want to pass your exams. Sometimes I wonder why I even bother."

Doodles threw his arms up in exasperation. "Riddley, I don't know what tests you're talking about and I don't know why I need to pass them!" As he said this, he realized that his voice echoed across the entire room. It was a weird sensation to hear his voice repeated back to him, reverberating off of the walls as if this were a cave.

Riddley didn't seem to be at all taken aback by Doodles raising his voice. It was as if he expected this reaction, and this only made Doodles even more upset.

"There are three tests, just as there are three knocks to enter. Didn't someone explain this to you?" Riddley's bushy eyebrows rose quizzically, and Doodles couldn't help but think the man looked like a wise, old owl.

He shook his head.

Riddley continued, "There are three knocks to enter my store. Three tests to pass to enter Inner Earth and three quests to complete to join the Masters." Riddley held up his hand knowing that Doodles would follow up with a question.

"Inner Earth is where aspiring Wizarts go to earn their Hats. Hats are symbols of Master Drawers. Each quest is more difficult than the last and is designed to prove a Wizart's ability. But—" Riddley held up three fingers and waved them. "No one can enter without passing the three tests."

Doodles tried to soak in this information. "Who are the masters?"

Riddley leaned forward, his back cracking audibly. "The book you read that told you where to go, that was made by a master. They are the elite of the Wizarts and they know the secrets of the world. They have mastered their art. Not many make it to that stage unfortunately. To them, most other Wizarts seem like kids with crayon or chalk."

"How am I to study for these tests if I don't know what they're about?" Doodles couldn't help but notice that Riddley kept his eyes on him at all times. In fact, he was sure that the old man had not blinked once since he had entered the bookstore.

"Whenever you draw, you get better. It is a matter of practice, my dear boy." Riddley rummaged through his pockets, all the while keeping his eyes on Doodles. He pulled out a small pocket watch and looked at the time. He sighed and put it back in his pocket.

"When do I take my first test then?" Doodles found himself sweating despite the cold. He was nervous, but he wanted answers. His whole life felt like a lie up until now. He knew deep in his heart that he wanted to find out more.

Riddley spoke with an authoritative tone, "Your first test begins now."

Doodles was the sort of kid who was always prepared for a test in school. He worked hard and his grades reflected his hard work. But here, in this situation, he had no control. In fact, he had no idea what he was about to be doing.

Riddley stood up to his full height. "I am going to draw something. The rules are simple and you must follow them. You can draw one item only. But be warned, what I am about to draw will try to sting you and it will hurt. So think carefully, but don't take too long."

"Wait, what?"

Before he could ask any more questions, Riddley picked up one of the brushes on the floor and began to paint.

Doodles panicked and ran over to grab another brush. He tried to slow his heart rate down so that he could focus.

Something that stung would probably be small, like a wasp or a bee. A sword like last time wouldn't help, and a net wouldn't do much good if they were too fast.

Think Doodles, think! he silently commanded himself.

"You're running out of time," Riddley warned.

Doodles quickly drew the next thing that came to his mind. He grabbed the vial of special black ink and painted over his drawing quickly. While Doodles was waiting for his drawing to come to life, Riddley's canvas gave a loud pop. He was too late.

Doodles couldn't have guessed further from the truth. Riddley had drawn a scorpion, and a big one at that.

The creature looked around the room and then locked onto Doodles. It began to crawl toward him.

He backed away holding onto his canvas.

"Come on, come on..." Doodles prayed. Those few seconds seemed to last forever.

The scorpion's eyes glowed fiery red, sunken into its head as if two dormant volcanoes waiting to erupt at any moment. It had scales, dark and hard as obsidian, covering its body from head to tail in seemingly impenetrable armor. Its movements were quick and deliberate and made a grating sound as its tail slid across the floor, scratching large grooves into the finely polished wood.

Just as the scorpion had backed Doodles into a corner there was a pop, and then a large metal box appeared. Doodles jumped inside and closed it up. The scorpion walked around the box testing its strength with its stinger with loud clanks against the metal side. Frustrated, the scorpion lost interest and turned toward Riddley.

Through the metal box, Doodles could barely hear Riddley's voice, muttering, "Uh-oh. Well that didn't go as planned."

By the time he got the courage to come out of the metal box, Riddley was huffing and puffing. "Don't ever do that again!" he shouted as he finished pouring some type of liquid on the scorpion. The creature now lay motionless on the wooden floor, half of its body no longer there.

"You're lucky I had some Dissolving Ink on me or else I would be in a world of pain." He let out a loud humph sound with his nostrils and straightened out his outfit to gain his composure. "Get out of here!"

Doodles didn't move at first. He was thankful that he wasn't stung, but concerned with Riddley's reaction. "Did I pass?" he asked as he moved toward the door.

Riddley's face turned bright red and he visibly focused on calming himself down. "Yes," he said at last. "You passed. You're the first one to give me a scare like that though. Pretty ingenious now that I come to think of it." The old man's smile returned and Doodles was thankful.

"Well go on. Don't stand here with a smart grin on your face. That was only one test of three and that was the easiest. Even though you passed, I am not pleased that you chose to hide from your challenge. You can't always go about life hiding, Doodles. You need to face your fears head on. I will see you tomorrow for the second test. Oh, and Doodles, don't forget to bring your own brush this time. A Wizart must always carry his or her own brush."

Doodles left with a smile on his face. He had passed the first test. He was closer to finding answers. For once in his life, he felt that his life meant something. This was exciting.

When he got home, his excitement left his body faster than the kids leave class when the bell rings. His mother was standing there with her arms crossed and a scowl that he knew all too well—he was late for dinner.

Doodles was grounded for the night. That meant no television, no leaving the house, and worst of all—no drawing.

His mother came into his room and gathered all of his art supplies up, mumbling the whole while about Doodles being irresponsible and disrespectful.

He would have normally been really upset, but he was still floating on a cloud. He had passed the first test. He was on his way to discovering more secrets. He could deal with his mom being mad at him for one night.

Tomorrow, he had a legitimate excuse to be late as he had his weekly chess club after school. Doodles didn't even want to go to the chess club any more, but he was thankful for the excuse it provided him. As there was nothing else to do, he was going to turn in and go to bed for the night when he heard a knock on his bedroom door. Three knocks.

Why were things happening in threes? What was so important about three? Doodles roused himself and shuffled over to the door. It was Uncle Roger. He wasn't too surprised. After all, his aunt and uncle lived only a few blocks away. They were always coming over, especially when his mother cooked some of her famously delicious meals.

"Hey Uncle Roger," Doodles said as he yawned sleepily.

"I heard you came home late tonight and didn't give an excuse as to why." He smiled and Doodles smiled back. He always found his uncle's smile to be contagious.

"Yeah," Doodles replied.

"Your mother needs to understand that you kids need time to get into mischief, so long as you aren't doing anything wrong. I'll have a talk with her." Uncle Roger yawned as well, stretching his arms out to the side.

Doodles suddenly caught a glimpse of his uncle's waistline. There, tucked into his belt was a long paintbrush. He had never known his uncle to paint anything. Did his uncle know about Wizartry? That seemed really unlikely. Although, come to think of it, anything seemed possible after his encounter at the bookstore.

He wanted to say something, but if he was wrong, he would sound like a complete dolt and possibly get into even more trouble than he was already in. He decided to wait until he knew more about everything before asking. His uncle smiled, patting Doodles on the head as if he were a good pup.

"Doodles, how is school going?" His uncle gave him a knowing look.

"Fine, Uncle Roger."

His uncle persisted, "How are your classmates treating you?"

Doodles knew that lying wouldn't get him anywhere with his uncle. He was sharper than he looked. "Not well," Doodles admitted reluctantly.

Uncle Roger nodded. "Remember to stay strong. Kids can be mean, but you have a big heart. You have a creative mind. Those qualities are rare. Things will get better, I promise."

Doodles stood there long after his uncle departed, all sorts of thoughts running through his head.

Chapter Four

THE PAINTBRUSH

School went by quickly. Laura insisted on coming with him to get a paintbrush after Doodles mentioned he was skipping chess club. She insisted she knew the best shop in town for paintbrushes. He didn't feel like arguing with her because it would have been more suspicious if he did. He figured he could ditch her at some point and rush over to Riddley's shop.

The paint store she brought him to was in close proximity to school on Bradley Street. It reminded Doodles of a picture from one of his history books with the old, cobbled walkways and streetlights that looked like antiques. It was quaint in its own way. His mother loved making his father take her for walks around the shops in Dockside on date nights.

As they walked, Doodles fought down the urge to hold her hand. At one point he accidently brushed her hand with his and pulled back. *What an idiot, I am!* he thought. She obviously thought of him as a friend. He knew he didn't have enough friends to risk ruining one of his best friendships.

Laura smiled at him as she pointed to an old building. It was two stories high with flowers of many brilliant colors carefully planted around the outside. Someone had taken great care of the little garden.

Doodles followed her inside.

She hadn't been exaggerating—the place was full from wall to wall with shelves of paintbrushes of all different styles and colors. There were packs of small and large brushes, boxes of assorted colors, and each one had distinct styles, length and size, and bristle design. It was almost overwhelming. Doodles couldn't believe he had never been here before.

When he asked her if it was a new shop she laughed at him and told him, "No, silly."

Laura walked right up to the counter as if she had been here before. "Hey Frank, this is my friend, Doodles. He's looking to buy a new paintbrush."

The man seemed friendly enough, and he was wearing a plain white, collared shirt and jeans. He leaned on the counter with his elbows, and when he recognized Laura, he stood up.

"Laura! Good to see you. You haven't been back here in quite a while—I was starting to think you forgot about us,"

Frank admonished jokingly, and then turned his attention to Doodles.

"What sort of brush are you looking for? Just one brush or a set? For acrylic paint or water based?"

Doodles chose his words carefully as to not draw any suspicion, not that they could guess what he was up to anyways. "Any brush will do." Thinking more about it he added, "Something sturdy."

"Aha, I see," Frank mumbled to himself as he looked through the shelf behind him. "No, not this one. This one is too flimsy—this one is too expensive. Here we are!" He turned around and handed a dark brown paintbrush to Doodles.

It was very nicely made, with polished, dark brown wood half the length of his forearm. The bristles were a dark grey color and looked like tiny needles standing packed tightly together. Doodles wasn't exactly sure what he wanted anyway, but this was impressive.

"How much?" he asked hesitantly, realizing he didn't have much cash in his pocket.

Frank looked at Laura and then back to Doodles. "Friends of Laura get their first brush free. She babysits my kid, after all. It's the least I can do for her." His friendly smile reminded Doodles a bit of his uncle.

"Thank you! I promise I'll put it to good use." Doodles hoped he was right.

He told Laura that he had to get home, and after he started to head in the right direction, he went back and headed toward Riddley's bookstore. He began to jog, fearing that he might be late again.

It was bright and sunny out today and Doodles whizzed by the shops and houses. He almost ran a lady over after turning a corner far too quickly. By the time he made it to the shop, it was already after five. Hopefully the test wouldn't take too long.

He went to knock three times like usual, but then stopped. He was certain this was the book shop. The bakers shop was right next door. There was the dumpster he had thrown the sword away in a few days ago. Then why was he standing in front of a brick wall? There was no door.

Doodles walked along the building thinking that maybe he had been mistaken. He couldn't find any doors or windows. This was extremely strange. Maybe he was too late, maybe Riddley had closed up shop, and then painted over the door with some sort of special paint so no one could bother him. Or perhaps Riddley had used Dissolving Ink on the door and painted a wall in its place. That would make sense.

He was too excited and had come too far just to go back home. He removed the paintbrush he had bought at the store with Laura and drew an outline of a door on the wall. Nothing happened. He didn't know why he thought he could draw something without any paint or any special ingredient to add to it. He stood there for a few minutes stubbornly and then turned around to head home. Then, there was a pop.

Doodles turned back around. There was a door just as he had drawn it, except for one minor problem. Instead of the doorknob, there was a giant goldfish. Doodles thought for a second, and then realized that Riddley had warned him about not using the correct amounts. He was surprised he had even been able to create a door without any paint or extras.

He walked up to the door, sure to stand wide of the goldfish, and then knocked three times. He waited. Just as before the door swung open.

Riddley stood on the other side, a confused look on his face. "It is really quite rude to draw a goldfish on someone else's door."

Doodles didn't know what to say, "I—"

Riddley laughed. "I'm just toying with you, Doodles. I'm surprised you made it this far. Most people fail the second test three times before passing, and most of the ones that pass finally get it into their thick skulls to go and buy some of their own paint. But you—you did it without any. While I appreciate the effort, I do so dislike a goldfish as my doorknob. Slimy and all, you know? Here, take this."

He handed Doodles some of his Dissolving Ink and after the door disappeared, Riddley insisted on drawing his own front door. "Ah, much better."

"What is today's test? I don't have too long as it is." Doodles looked around to see if he could get any clues to what would happen next.

"That was it. You passed. You made it inside. Now don't go bragging about it either. Just because you made it look easy doesn't mean it was." He reached into his pocket and pulled out a coin.

It took a moment for everything to sink in for Doodles. "Okay, so tomorrow is the final test then?"

Riddley shook his head. "No. You're moving too quickly. I need to teach you more before you're even close to ready to face the dangers of Inner Earth. I have an assignment for you. You will have one week to complete it and in that time you must be ready for anything."

He placed the coin in Doodles' palm. "This coin is your access to the final test. Keep it with you for the week. Then, return it to the store and hand it to me and you can take your test. But be warned. This coin attracts all sorts of people who will want to take it away from you. Its powers will test your resolve and creativity. Never let your guard down."

Doodles looked down at it. This was going to be a long week.

Doodles looked at the coin periodically throughout the school day to make sure it was still in his pocket. He didn't think this test was going to be that difficult. He just had to make sure he steered clear of anyone that might take it from him. He found himself running from class to class just to make sure.

Two days passed this way, and nothing out of the ordinary happened. Doodles began to let his guard down. This was going to be easier than he thought.

At lunch on the third day, he was listening to Darren babble on about some sort of natural disaster he saw on the news when suddenly Brandon was standing next to him.

"What are you guys talking about?" Brandon asked, pretending to be interested.

Darren stopped talking and went about eating his food. This must have been difficult for him—turning off his mouth after it started moving was no easy task.

Jimmy slunk down and tried to make himself even smaller.

"Oh, hey, Elf. How rude of me not to say hi to you," he laughed.

"Shut up, Brandon," Laura snarled as she stared menacingly at him. "Go bother someone else."

Brandon ignored her and turned his attention on Doodles. "Doodles, been a long time since you gave me lunch money. Cough it up."

He swallowed hard. He didn't have any money. The only thing he had in his pocket was the coin Riddley had given him. There were no teachers around and he definitely could not win a fight or outrun Brandon. Brandon was on both the wrestling and track teams. That combination made him a strong and fierce enemy.

"I don't have anything," Doodles lied, trying to buy some more time to think.

Brandon leaned in closer to him. "You're lying. I'm only going to ask one more time."

Doodles was about to run for it when Laura pushed her way between them. She looked up at Brandon and said, "If you don't leave right now, I swear to God, Brandon Smith, that I will spread a rumor to the entire school about how you wet your pants."

Brandon looked at her in surprise, and then swallowed. "Whatever. You losers aren't worth it."

As he walked away, Doodles let out a sigh of relief. "I can't believe that worked."

Laura laughed. "If there's one thing I know about Brandon, it's that he will do anything to keep his reputation."

Doodles was in a foul mood now. He decided to take the long way home to clear his head. Not only did he almost lose the coin, but he also relied on Laura to stand up for him. Any small chance that he thought he had with her was gone now. Not that it mattered anyway. Girls like Laura were way out of his league.

Doodles kicked a particularly large rock and nearly cursed as he stubbed his toe. He found a wooden bench and sat down for a minute to calm down. It always seemed to Doodles that whenever he thought his life was getting better, it turned south.

As he sat there, another man came and sat next to him. Doodles normally wouldn't have paid any attention to a stranger, but the man sat uncomfortably close on the more than spacious bench.

"Um…can I help you?" he asked, leaning away from the newcomer.

The man was looking right at him. "Your coin, can I have it?"

Doodles jumped up at this and then noticed something—the man was wearing an odd hat.

"How did you know?" He backed slowly away from the stranger, keeping his hand close to his brush.

"I wouldn't do that if I were you," the man warned as he brought out his own brush and laid it casually across his lap. "Now where were we? Oh yes, you were about to give me your coin."

"How did you know about it?"

Doodles was really frightened now. The hat and the brush made sense. This man was a Wizart, and according to the hat, it meant he was a master one at that, the first one he met other than Riddley.

"What? Did you think all Wizarts are nice? Far from it. I mean, why should we be? You dare to walk around with a Calling Coin as casually as you are and think nothing will come of it?"

"Calling Coin?"

The man laughed condescendingly. "You're naïve then. I was hoping you were simply dumb. I might as well explain what I'm about to take from you so that it hurts all the more. You see, Calling Coins are sought after by everyone who knows how valuable they are. An artist can store a drawing for later use and activate it with the coin. They are made from deep in Inner Earth which makes them so rare they are worth more than a mountain of gold. Fortunately, the metal gives off a distinct signal that people like me know to look for. I'm done talking. Hand it over and I'll let you live."

Doodles thought for a moment, and then took his brush out. He quickly started to draw.

"You fool!" the man yelled as he stood up and began to draw as well. He was so fast that Doodles was sure he must be really skilled.

Pop! A sword appeared in the stranger's hand. "Don't move," he said as he approached, reaching for Doodles' pocket.

Little did the man know that Doodles had finished his drawing as well. Pop!

"Why am I standing in the middle of the street?" Riddley yelled as he appeared between the man and Doodles with a fork and knife in his hands. "And how dare you draw me when I am in the middle of dinner!"

"And you, Alanso!" Riddley stuck the fork toward the man's chest, unafraid of the sword pointed at him. "You'd better leave at once or consider it your last trip to Inner Earth, so help me!"

Doodles had never heard Riddley this angry. Despite his frail body, he seemed confident and authoritative.

The man named Alanso gave a warning look to Doodles and Doodles held his breath as he wondered if the man would try something regardless of Riddley's warning. The moment seemed to last forever, and just like that, Alanso mumbled some sort of curse and walked away. Looking back one last time he said, "I'm not through with you yet, Doodles."

Riddley watched to make sure Alanso had left and then turned back toward Doodles. "Congratulations. You just made an enemy of one of the most powerful Wizarts out there, spoiled my dinner, and nearly broke the rules of the assignment all in a few minutes. Don't ever draw me again!"

Doodles dropped his gaze, "I'm sorry. I panicked when he tried to attack me."

Riddley sighed. "I've never had a student try that before. How did you know it would even work?" He stared down at Doodles with a stern look in his eyes. "What did I tell you when you passed your first test? I told you that you have to face your fears on your own. Someone might not always be there to save you. You can't go about life hiding or expecting someone to bail you out of all your troubles. You are on your own until Friday. Be more careful next time."

With that, Riddley headed off, muttering under his breath.

Doodles didn't stick around in case Alanso came back.

Doodles did what any other teenager does to get out of trouble—he pretended to be sick. His mom stayed home from work in order to take care of him, and honestly, Doodles didn't mind the attention. He had been scared all the way down to his bones after his encounter with Alanso. Not only had he had a sword pointed at him, but he had made an enemy of one of the strongest Wizarts. It was a terrifying thought.

He had stayed in bed for two days straight, not daring to get up except to use the bathroom. He had even gone so far as to lock the window and tie it with some rope he found in the garage. Not that a window could stop a Wizart like Alanso if he found out where he lived. Doodles thought back to when he drew that door on Riddley's shop. If Doodles could do that with no experience…Doodles swallowed and tried to think about something else.

Laura stopped by to wish him well. She had heard he was out sick. It was really nice to have such a caring friend.

Doodles tried to focus on that but it was useless. He was getting anxious the more he lay in bed and time seemed to speed up and slow down in pace with his heartbeat.

This afternoon, it was time to turn the coin over to Riddley, if he could even make it there. Doodles almost considered the idea of simply handing the coin over to Alanso. Was all of this worth it? The thought of learning more secrets and seeing Inner Earth was too much to pass up. Doodles had waited his entire life for a moment like this.

Doodles had time, laying there in his bed, to think about a strategy to get him to the book store without getting caught. He played over the different routes in his head and in each scenario, he imagined Alanso popping up out of nowhere. There were too many things that could go wrong.

And then a smile crossed Doodles' face as he thought of a plan.

Chapter Five

THE ROAD TO DANGER

A boy with dark black hair walked down the street, covered from head to toe in unassuming dark clothes. He walked quickly, knowing exactly which alleyway to walk down and every shadow to hide in. His face was covered in freckles and half-hidden behind the hoodie he wore.

Someone who followed the boy would have trouble keeping up as the boy darted down alleyways and hopped over fences, always moving quickly. After a good half-hour, the boy arrived in front of a building and opened the door.

"Oh, hello, can I help you?" Riddley asked, getting up from his chair.

The boy stood there and smiled. He held out his hand to display a glowing, blue coin.

Riddley took the coin and then eyed the boy. His eyebrows furrowed curiously and then relaxed as recognition crossed his face. "Doodles! You made it! I almost didn't recognize you. That was quite a clever plan you came up with."

Doodles was so happy to get the coin out of his hands that he let out the largest sigh he ever had. It felt as if a lead weight had been lifted off of his shoulders. "This has been the longest week of my life."

Riddley nodded his understanding, "You did well, except for using me as defense against Alanso. Remember, one day, you will have to face your fears on your own. That aside, I believe you are ready for the third and final test."

Doodles' ears perked up. This was it. This is what would gain him access to even more secrets. "What's the third test?"

Riddley thought for a moment and then spoke, his voice thoughtful. "Normally, I would give you the standard test, but you have proven to be a quicker learner than most. As such, I need to think of a fitting test, one that will prove your creativity, heart, and resolve. I will need a day to prepare. In the meantime, you have earned yourself some Dissolving Ink, one vial to be exact, and some Heart Liquid. The Heart liquid is the most prized possession any Wizart can have, aside from his brush of course. The liquid is made from the pollen of the Alaka plant deep within Inner Earth. I trust you will use this responsibly. Don't go around painting over stop signs and making them disappear. While this is quite amusing, it is highly frowned upon." He leaned forward, his bushy eyebrows furled at the end. "And it would be a shame to waste such precious liquid."

Doodles nodded. "Why do they call it Heart Liquid?"

"The name serves dual purposes. First being that it is literally from the center or heart of the Alaka plant and second that any drawing requires a heartbeat to come alive. We are just the painters, while the Heart Liquid is the catalyst to bring it to life."

Riddley stood back up and stretched. "Well, you know the drill. Out with you and don't come back until tomorrow afternoon." Riddley almost pushed him out of the door this time.

～

Doodles almost forgot to paint himself back to normal. He didn't know how he'd talk himself out of that situation. He was turning the corner to his house when he saw Uncle Roger sitting on the front porch. Doodles wondered how long he'd been waiting there.

"Hey, Uncle Roger," Doodles said. "Is everything okay?"

Uncle Roger motioned for Doodles to sit. "We need to talk."

Doodles had never seen his uncle this quiet except for when he was eating. His uncle was usually upbeat and constantly making jokes. In this moment, however, he was more serious than Doodles had ever seen him. This notion was strange and somewhat scary for him. He wanted to run away, to avoid whatever it was that was troubling his uncle so much.

After a few moments, Doodles did as his uncle asked.

What is this about? Am I in trouble? he wondered.

"I haven't always been honest with you. I don't know where to begin." Roger shifted his weight and scratched his ear nervously. "There is no easy way to say this and so I'll just cut to the chase. I know you have been training under Riddley. It was no accident that your aunt and I gave you the book. We were waiting until your thirteenth birthday. You see, that's when all aspiring Wizarts try out for access to Inner Earth. There are things you have learned recently and so many things you don't know. I wish I could tell you more..." he trailed off and looked toward the sky.

Doodles sat there quietly, trying to absorb as much as he could.

Uncle Roger continued, "Your parents aren't Wizarts, but they know about our kind. You don't have to hide this from us anymore." He finally locked eyes with Doodles. "I spoke with Riddley. I know your last test is tomorrow and I want you to understand how important it is that you pass."

Doodles finally spoke, "I'm just happy there's finally someone I can talk to about this."

Uncle Roger nodded. "Yes, that must feel nice. But understand this—there are many people counting on you. Inner Earth is in trouble and someone with your talents could help save it."

"What do you mean trouble?"

Uncle Roger lowered his voice. "I can't tell you until you pass. But it's vital that you *do* pass."

"But why me? I don't even know that much," Doodles protested.

"You've been practicing your whole life. You were born with a special talent. Riddley hasn't told you the whole truth—ninety-nine percent of Wizarts who try to pass the three tests fail for at least a few years. The point of the series of tests is to show growth and the ability to learn. You have passed two in a matter of a week. The last person that did that was years ago. His name was Alanso."

At the mention of that name, Doodles caught his breath and nearly choked.

Uncle Roger went on, "Inner Earth is in trouble Doodles, grave and serious trouble. They need you."

Minutes later, Doodles found himself in his living room, surrounded by his aunt, uncle, mother, and father with all eyes focused on him. This was a familiar place with people he normally felt at ease with, but nothing about this situation was comfortable.

"I don't see why Riddley can't just let me in then. If Inner Earth is really in that great a danger and I'm supposedly the only one that can help, why can't we just go right now?" Doodles asked. He knew it couldn't be that easy, but he felt like he had to ask.

His family looked at each other as if wondering who would answer first. Finally his aunt spoke up. "Sweetie, it isn't as simple as that. There are rules."

His father added, "She's right. Rules are rules, and if we went around breaking them, well, everything might turn to chaos."

"But it's just Riddley! He can make the test easier for me just this once, can't he?" Doodles looked around hopefully.

His mother shook her head, "Honey, it's not just Riddley. The third test is performed in front of the Gate

Council. They are the ones who vote whether or not a student gains access to Inner Earth."

"How many are there?" Doodles asked.

"Three, and they are the strictest, by-the-book members who have ever sat on the council," Uncle Roger said.

"We can't plead our case to them?" Doodles suggested.

Uncle Roger answered, "It wouldn't do any good. We have already asked. The best we could do was make them promise us they would give you a vote tomorrow. In fact, the main issue stems from your age. Although you are right on the borderline for eligibility, some of the council members think it is customary to be somewhat older. They have been known to be rigid in their ways. The typical age is fifteen. We will have to wait and see what they say and hope for the best." He shrugged, his massive shoulders slumping in resignation.

"What happens tomorrow? How can I prepare?" Doodles started to bite his fingernails nervously. It was a bad habit he gave in to when he found himself in extremely stressful situations.

Doodles' family avoided making eye contact with him. For the first time in his life, he felt distant from his own family.

Finally, his uncle spoke up, "We couldn't tell you even if we knew. All we can tell you is to open your mind, stay true to your heart, and never give up. Riddley told me about your tests. It's time to grow up and believe in yourself. It's time to stop hiding and running. You're more talented than you think."

Doodles gulped. He knew what his uncle was saying should give him more confidence, but it only proved to add more pressure.

Doodles couldn't sleep—this was all happening so fast. Just a few weeks ago, he was some loser with no real talent. All at once, he discovered that he had magical talents and not only that, but people were relying on him.

Maybe he should practice for tomorrow's test. He hopped down from his bed, rummaged in his sock drawer, pulled out his paintbrush, and then took a seat on the floor. He wasn't sure what the test would be tomorrow.

As he thought about his life and the difficulties that lay ahead of him, he absentmindedly began to paint. This was no strange task for Doodles. He had spent hours in his room drawing ever since he was little.

Pop! A creature appeared in front of Doodles. He hurriedly backed away from what appeared to be a big ball of fluff about the size of a golden retriever, with bright blue fur and large, oval eyes. It had short, stubby arms, and its feet were very much like a penguin's.

Doodles was about to yell, when suddenly, the creature spoke.

"Hello."

Doodles jumped at the sound.

"You can talk?"

"Well of course I can talk. You drew me, after all." The creature waddled closer and sniffed loudly with its large nostrils. "Pleasure to meet you. I would shake your hand but someone I know—and I'm not naming names—neglected to draw hands for me." The thing, whatever it was, did indeed only have a ball of fluff at the end of his stubby arms.

"Oh, I'm sorry," Doodles muttered awkwardly.

"Well, there's no sense in apologizing now. The name's Boogley. Nice to meet you."

"Doodles. My name is Doodles."

"What kind of a name is that? " The creature smiled to reveal a set of pointy teeth.

Doodles wanted to ask what kind of name was Boogley but he thought better of it, especially after seeing those chompers.

"Well, Boogley, I was busy practicing for a test tomorrow. I don't suppose you have any advice?"

He waddled around the room a bit more and sniffed at Doodles' shoes. "These are foul smelling. You should wash them."

Doodles smiled abashedly—he was really starting to like this thing. "Do you know anything about the Wizartry Council?"

Boogley stopped sniffing and looked up. "The council? You do know I was created today, right? The only things I've seen are a depressed-looking kid and some stinky shoes."

"Yeah, I don't know why I assumed you knew something," Doodles replied, as his shoulders slumped and he leaned against the side of his bed. "I'm going to fail tomorrow if I don't do something about it." He placed his head into his hands and tried to think.

"Hey, now! Don't do that! It makes me get all teary-eyed when I see someone so sad. . Then I can't see at all and go bumping into all sorts of walls and such. Why do you think you are going to fail?"

Doodles looked up and tried to regain his composure. "There's too much pressure. I don't even know what I'm facing."

"Then how do you know you'll fail? Seems silly to me that you think you can predict the future."

Doodles thought about it for a minute. "I guess you're right, but I can't help but feel overwhelmed with it all."

"It seems like a natural feeling to me to worry. But it doesn't mean you have to feel powerless. You drew *me* after all. Pretty creative if I say so myself. Don't dwell on all the bad stuff. You have your creativity. That's all you really need."

"Thank you, Boogley. What are you going to do?"

"I suppose I could come with you and support you. Not much else to do."

Doodles laughed. "I would love that."

Knowing his family was there in attendance didn't really help the nervousness Doodles felt. In fact, it made it worse knowing they were relying on him. He didn't know where he was or how he'd gotten here—he'd been blindfolded on the way over, and it certainly wasn't Riddley's bookstore. The location of the Wizartry council was to remain secret until he became a full-fledged Wizart and earned his hat.

He removed his blindfold. There was a fairly large crowd of spectators seated around a circular, stone area. The rows of seats were very high up, giving the onlookers a clear view of the stone area and the adjacent rooms from above. Doodles stood in the middle of the stone tiles and scanned the audience, searching for signs of his family. He thought he caught a glimpse of Riddley, but he couldn't be certain it was him, as the room was dark and the stands were so high up.

The only lighting was provided by three torches placed an equal distance apart across the room. It would be nice to know that Riddley was here supporting him. He knew Boogley was here because he had come with them.

Mrs. Lanhorn had argued that Boogley would tear up the car seats, but after some convincing and negotiating, Boogley was allowed to sit in the far back seat. Boogley had talked the entire way. Although Doodles' parents felt somewhat awkward about a creature with pointy teeth the size of a medium-sized dog sitting behind them, it kept everyone's minds off of what lay ahead.

Behind the torches sat two men and a woman who Doodles assumed were the council members his uncle had referred to. They all wore similar black robes, their heads adorned with elaborate hats, twice as large as any of the audience members' hats. Their faces were serious and their gazes were locked onto Doodles. For the minute or so after Doodles' blindfold was off, not one of the council members spoke. It was an awkward and terrifying feeling. The crowd muttered restlessly until the woman spoke, her voice immediately silencing the room.

"I am council member Holly. We are gathered here for the final test for access to Inner Earth. For the record, please announce your name to the witnesses."

He tried to stand up straight but it just made him feel more awkward. "My name is Doodles Lanhorn."

Holly nodded and gestured to the man on her right.

He, in turn, jotted something down on a piece of paper and cleared his throat. "Welcome, Doodles Lanhorn. I am Charles, the eldest of the council members and note taker of all council affairs. Today you will have the third and final test in front of the council and witnesses who will—"

Charles was interrupted by the last council member. "How old is he? He can't be old enough—look at him!"

Charles seemed unbothered by the interruption and continued, "That is a fair question, Brian. How old are you, Doodles Lanhorn?"

Doodles thought about lying in order to ensure he was allowed to take the test, but then thought better of it. "I just turned thirteen, sir."

The spectators reacted and began to talk in hushed voices. Holly held up her hand for silence and they instantly quieted. She spoke, "There is no set age. They are merely guidelines. You remember Alanso don't you?"

"He was thirteen and a half! And even that is far too early," Brian replied.

Holly shook her head. "Half a year makes no difference. I say we vote if he should be allowed to take the final test. All in favor raise your hands."

The room went completely silent as Holly raised her hand. She was the only one. Doodles gulped. He was out-voted two to one.

He couldn't believe it—he had come so close, and now he had not only failed at moving on, he had let his entire family down. He was about to thank them for their time when suddenly a voice rang out. He recognized that voice. It was Riddley.

"Hold it one minute!" Riddley called out as he stumbled past two people and into the center.

"What is the meaning of this?" Brian stammered angrily.

Riddley walked right up to the front of the council members and took off his hat. "You all know who I am, correct?"

"Get to your point," Brian said gruffly.

"You all agree I have passed my tests and quests and have become a full-fledged Wizart?" Riddley stood confidently in front of the council members.

"Yes, of course. What does that have to do with—?" Brian began to speak.

Holly cut him off. "Go on, Riddley."

Riddley cleared his throat dramatically. "Then, as such, I reserve the right to risk my reputation by taking on Doodles as his sponsor."

There was another eruption from the crowd.

Holly leaned forward. "You realize what you're asking? As a sponsor, if Doodles fails his test you will also be kicked out of Inner Earth, but by being his sponsor you allow him to take the test based on your reputation. It's written in the laws that you may do this."

Riddley nodded his understanding. "I know the risk. If it means he can take the test, then let's get on with it."

Holly hid a smile. She continued, "Very well, then it's settled. There can be no argument. Doodles Lanhorn will take the final test with Riddley as his sponsor."

Riddley leaned toward Doodles and whispered into his ear, "You'd better pass."

The crowd quieted down. The room was so silent that Doodles could hear his own heartbeat. He could feel sweat starting to form on his forehead as he waited apprehensively. Not only did he have his family relying on him, and apparently the fate of Inner Earth, but now Riddley was counting on him as well.

Council member Charles scribbled something on a piece of paper and put his pen down. He cleared his throat. "The test will consist of three rooms. In each room you will meet with one of us. The goal in each room is to find and pick up the Calling Coin. Understand?"

Doodles nodded.

"Good. Then if there is nothing further..." Charles turned to Holly, who in turn nodded her consent. The three council members departed. Doodles was sure that the council member named Brian gave him one final dirty look before exiting through a wooden door on the far side of the room. The crowd began to talk excitedly and Doodles was starting to become even more nervous. What was in each room? Hopefully Riddley had trained him well enough to expect the unexpected.

Doodles took a deep breath and opened the door. Stepping into the first room he was happy to see it was Holly. She seemed to be the nicest of the three.

Holly took out a Calling Coin from her pocket and tossed it on the floor in front of her. Doodles was about to run forward when he looked down. There were patterns on the floor, strange colors and shapes that looked suspicious. Doodles took out his brush and drew a handful of pebbles. All the while Holly watched in silence. When the pebbles appeared in his hand, Doodles took one and tossed it a few feet in front of him. It landed on a red tile and began to sink. It was quicksand! Doodles took another pebble out and tossed it onto a blue tile. It fell through the floor as if the tile wasn't even there. Doodles found a green tile and tossed the last pebble. His aim was spot on and it bounced across the green tile. Doodles waited, but nothing happened. So the green tiles were safe.

The only problem was that the green tiles were spaced far apart. He jumped to the first, and then the second and third. He really had to strain himself on the last couple, and almost lost his balance a few times. The tiles were large, but not large enough for an awkward teen.

Bending down he picked up the Calling Coin and put it into his pocket.

"Well done Doodles. You may enter the next room," Holly said as she smiled. Her smile reminded Doodles of Laura from school. Laura's smile could always make him feel better despite what was going on. Doodles wondered if Laura was worried about where he was. Did she even notice? Of course she did. His thoughts were interrupted as the crowd clapped excitedly from high above and Doodles couldn't help but gain more confidence. He was almost there. Holly graciously stepped aside and allowed Doodles to step through the doorway.

In the next room, Doodles was met by Charles. Just like the last room, Charles stood at the very end of the room. He also took out a Calling Coin and tossed it onto the floor. Only this time, as opposed to the prior room with council member Holly, Charles began to paint. Doodles grabbed his brush in preparation. Unfortunately, there was nothing Doodles could do or paint because he wouldn't know what to draw until he saw what Charles had created first. Charles moved surprisingly fast despite his age, and it was difficult to make out from across the room what he was creating.

Charles stopped painting and took a step back, his arms crossed behind his back casually. Doodles readied his muscles to act. The anticipation made sweat drip down his neck. His grip tightened on the paintbrush.

A metal cage appeared around the Calling Coin. It looked like it was made out of thick iron bars. The gap between the bars was far too tight for Doodles to fit his hands or arms through. Doodles approached the cage. Just then a contraption appeared-a rather rudimentary trap. A metal pole stood on top of the cage with four rods hanging down on either side of the cage. A heavy wooden log swung back and forth on all sides of the cage. Doodles watched and calculated. There was roughly five seconds between each swing. Not much time to reach the coin.

Doodles began to paint. He created a fishing pole with a sticky substance on which he hoped would stick to the coin, if he could get it. It sounded like a good plan in theory, but Doodles was nervous that if gym class was any indication of his athleticism and hand-eye coordination, he was in trouble. Doodles readied the fishing pole and watched the wooden log swing back and forth methodically. He let the log pass and ran forward. Doodles stuck the fishing pole through the bars and aimed for the coin. He was so nervous that his hands shook and he missed the coin several times. Out of the corner of his eye he caught the log coming back and he jumped back. The log nearly got his shoulder.

Doodles stood up and took a deep breath. If he was to do this, he needed to calm himself down so that his hands could be steady when reaching for the coin. *You can do this Doodles,* he silently affirmed. He waited again for the log to pass and leapt forward. He pictured himself drawing on the floor of his room, a scene he was comfortable and familiar with. His hand remained steady just like when he drew late at night. The sticky substance fell onto the coin and with a tug, Doodles pulled and fell back. The wooden log flew by where he had just been. He fell onto the floor and awkwardly rolled to a sitting position. He grabbed the Calling Coin quickly and placed it in his pocket. *Two coins down. Just one more to go,* he thought.

Charles nodded and pointed towards the door leading to the last room. "The last room is yours to enter. Be careful."

Doodles brushed dust off of his pants and walked carefully into the next room. Again he was met with loud cheering from high above in the audience.

Council member Brian was in the final room. He stood there with a sinister grin on his face. Doodles wasn't sure why Brian seemed to hate him. He hadn't done anything to him that Doodles knew of.

"So you made it to my room-beginner's luck. Now for a real test." Brian tossed the Calling Coin onto the floor and pressed a red button on the wall before exiting quickly through the back door. Doodles felt the walls and ground tremble suddenly. His whole body began to shake from the vibrations.

Water began gushing into the room from several openings. Doodles took out his brush only to have it swept away in the current. Doodles was also swept off of his feet. All he could do was to keep himself from going under the water. His arms were growing tired and the brush and Calling Coin were now below five feet of water. The water level continued to rise and Doodles began to panic. Doodles ducked his head under water and saw the coin. He tried to swim towards it but the current was too strong. Without his brush, there was nothing he could do.

It can't end here. It just can't. I've come too far.
Doodles began to trace fins with his hands. He didn't know why
he thought this would work. It was told to him by Riddley and
every other Wizart that Wizartry required both a paintbrush and
Heart Liquid. He had neither. Yet he continued to try all the
same. Just like in class, faint lights appeared where his hands
moved. He concentrated even harder. The light and lines
became more solid.

Suddenly the fins appeared. Doodles quickly put them
on, making sure the water did not wash them away. It was much
easier to swim now. He dove under the water and swam towards
the Calling Coin. Grabbing the coin, Doodles swam to the
surface and pushed the red button on the wall on the way up.
The water receded. Doodles stood there shivering and drenched.

The crowd was silent. There were no cheers this time.
Doodles looked at his hands in shock. *How had he done that?*

He'd just broken all of the rules of magic and drew
something without even a brush, let alone using any paint.

The council members filed into the room. They
looked at Doodles in shock. Finally, after what seemed like an
eternity to Doodles, council member Holly spoke, "Doodles
Lanhorn, you're hereby granted rights to enter Inner Earth. We
obviously want to look more into the powers you have just
shown, but unfortunately we do not have the luxury of time.
When you return, and hopefully successfully, we will need to

study what you have done more closely. We've never seen someone able to draw without use of a brush. Wizartry has been around for thousands of years, and not once is this skill mentioned. I am proud to task you with your first quest to earn your hat and your place as a full-fledged Wizart." Even council member Brian nodded.

Doodles smiled uncertainly, "What's the quest?"

Holly continued, her voice growing more intense. "It's best that you say goodbye to your loved ones just in case you don't make it out of there alive. What you face in Inner Earth is much more deadly than what we tasked you with today. Someone has cast a horrific spell which has spread and poisoned all the waters in Inner Earth. Life is dying there. The normally beautiful forests and enchanted animals are poisoned and no one can seem to find the source of this blasphemy. We have named it the Eraser. Find it and destroy it."

"I'll try my best." Doodles tried to sound hopeful, but he knew his voice must've sounded far from it. "But why me? Why a thirteen-year-old kid instead of any number of fully trained Wizarts around the world?"

Holly's voice softened. "Because most Wizarts have been called away for the Wizartry conference in northern England. It is most certainly not happenstance that the Eraser started during the Wizartry conference. Whoever did this, they knew this would be the prime opportunity to unleash this foul spell."

Charles scratched his balding head. "You aren't the only one we are going to send, and you aren't the first. There were a few Wizarts that did not attend the conference. No one has succeeded in stopping the Eraser yet. Although this is the first time you have met us, Riddley and your Uncle Roger have described in great detail the talent you possess. Now that you have shown that you can do things no other Wizart can, perhaps there is hope in you to succeed where others have failed."

Brian spoke, "We have recalled many of our most talented Wizarts from the conference. They may not make it here in time. There is a great storm delaying all methods of travel in England. Unfortunately, you are our last hope." He shook his head. "To think we would place all of our hopes in a thirteen-year old boy…"

Doodles looked towards the audience. "Why can't Riddley go? He's skilled and he's here."

Holly shook her head. "Riddley must stay to guard the entrance to Inner Earth. Rules have to be abided by."

His family was suddenly beside him. They must have come down while he was talking to the council members. He hugged his mother and father in one embrace. "I'm scared," he whispered to his mother.

"I know, sweetie. Just remember, with hard work, most things tend to work out in the end. You'll be fine, I just know it. You're more talented than anyone I've ever seen." Mrs. Lanhorn gave him a loving look as tears began to cloud her eyes.

His uncle gave him a bear hug, scooping him up into his huge arms. "You be strong."

Doodles nodded. His aunt tried to give a pleasant smile, opened her mouth to say something, and then stopped. This was the first time Doodles had seen her speechless.

Lastly, he turned to his father who stood there grinning. "I'm so proud of you for what you accomplished and who you're becoming." Doodles looked down at his hands. He never would have thought that, one day, they could create something without the use of paint or brushes.

Riddley placed his arm on Doodles' shoulder. "Hurry to wherever it is you must go. And whatever you do, when you enter Inner Earth, no matter what, under no circumstances should you let your guard down. Treat everyone and everything as a potential enemy. Use your creativity and your heart and face your problems. No more hiding. Keep in mind that there are thousands of defenseless magical and exotic creatures in Inner Earth. Most importantly, the sacred lands of Inner Earth are home to Wizart retirees as well as the Heart Liquid. Without the Heart Liquid, Wizartry will disappear forever!" Riddley leaned closer so that only Doodles could hear. "Whatever the Eraser is, it is a powerful and evil spell. Find it and get rid of it at all costs. Well, what are you waiting for? Go on then," he said as he made a shooing motion with his hands. "Plenty of customers back at the store waiting for me."

Doodles never got to ask the hundreds of questions he had floating around in his head. The council members led him to a wall at the far end of the room.

Charles pointed to the wall and Doodles could now make out a faint outline of a door. "Trace the outline exactly. Do not add any other details. No need to be fancy here. The spell is an ancient one and requires precision. This has been the entryway to Inner Earth since the first Wizart appeared hundreds of years ago. Once you have painted it, add the Heart Liquid and the door will appear. The rest is up to you."

Doodles' hand was surprisingly steady as he painted. It only took a few minutes and the door appeared. He stepped through the door toward Inner Earth without looking back. It would have been too hard to see his family again. Unbeknownst to Doodles, Boogley waddled after him, managing to slip through the doorway before it closed.

Chapter Six

Inner Earth

Doodles took a few steps after closing the door to Inner Earth behind him and then tumbled forward. He landed on what felt like a slanted cave wall covered in inches of thickly growing moss. It was slimy to his touch and he could not slow his decent. *What if I fall forever?* Doodles thought. *What if I land on rocks?* Just as he was about ready to cry out for help, his descent stopped and he landed on a stone floor. Luckily the slope had gone up slightly at the end, somewhat hindering his fall.

Doodles could barely see in the darkness. He shivered suddenly. There was a wind coming from somewhere. Doodles quickly started to move his hands to draw. The lights his hands created allowed him to see in the darkness. He drew a flashlight, then took ahold of it and turned it on. He shivered again. Looking around, he was able to see that he was in a cave. From as far as the flashlight would allow him to see, the cave must have been at least fifty feet tall. The encroaching darkness reminded him of the drawings he used to make for Laura.

Shivering again, Doodles decided to draw a sweater and quickly pulled it on. He really was alone now. Riddley wasn't here to help, and his friends and family were far away. It was just him, Doodles Lanhorn. He studied the cave as he walked. The ground was damp and sloped downwards. As he walked, he realized that the cave might go on for miles. There was no way to keep track of what time of day it was down here. It felt as though he must have walked a mile already.

The wind was picking up and it was clear that it was coming from further ahead. Doodles missed his family in this moment, alone and cold in a cave deep within the Earth. He missed Pancake Saturdays most of all. But this is what he had wanted. His whole life he knew something was different about him. This was a real adventure, and Doodles intended to succeed. It was getting colder as he made his way further into Inner Earth.

He was just about ready to sit down and take a break when he saw a light ahead. It was faint, but it was definitely a light. With the promise of an end to this journey, Doodles continued, his energy renewed.

Before he knew it, he stood before a large cave opening. Looking out, he had to shield his eyes from the brightness of a sun. A large sun illuminated the sky, and he saw clouds and trees, and miles and miles of grass. Doodles thought that this was impossible. It looked just like the sun he knew, only smaller. It was as if they were in a giant dome and the sun was a hazy yellow-green sun. It was not only beautiful, but unbelievable. His mind tried to grasp the whole concept of what his eyes were seeing. How was there all of this deep within the Earth? It was like a world inside of a world. How had scientists not discovered this yet? Doodles remembered the doorway he had to draw in order to enter Inner Earth. Maybe that was why no one aside from Wizarts has been here.

Doodles breathed in the fresh air, and almost forgot his troubles for a minute. He enjoyed the view of rolling hills and fields and felt the breeze on his face. Just then, there was a shout, a woman's voice calling out for help, bringing Doodles back to reality.

The screams became more desperate and he quickly took off, running down a hill at full speed toward the sound. Whoever it was, it sounded like they were in trouble. The screams grew louder and more intense as he approached a forest's edge. The trees had bright purple leaves, just like in the book his uncle and aunt had given him.

Doodles dodged trees and jumped over rocks until he burst through a copse and into a clearing. There he came across a woman running toward him at full speed. She nearly bowled him over as he caught her in his arms.

"What's wrong?" Doodles asked trying to calm her down.

She looked up at him, clearly out of breath and pointed to the far side of the clearing she had just come from.

"They're after…me…with sharp fangs…and…" She gulped in more air and continued, "They must have drunk some…of that water because they…are berserk." She shrieked suddenly and stood behind Doodles as three large wolves came crashing through the brush on the far side of the clearing.

The woman was leaning heavily on Doodles' arm, clearly not in a position to run anymore. She must have been running for quite some time. She took out her paintbrush.

"Where's your…brush?" she said, panting between words.

"I don't need one," Doodles replied.

She gave him a confused look.

Doodles didn't hesitate. As the wolves charged, he started to draw with his hand. The woman watched him, baffled as he danced waving his arms around.

"Well if you're not…going to…do anything," she said as she quickly drew a cage around herself. The wolves were close enough now that they opened their mouths in anticipation of food, spittle visibly dripping from their gaping mouths.

The woman watched in horror through her cage as the wolves approached Doodles at a breakneck pace. "Do something! If you don't have a brush, then run!" she yelled in fear.

Doodles finished and stood back. A wall of sticky webbing appeared, stretching ten feet across. He stood behind the tangled mess and jumped up and down, screaming in order to draw the attention of the wild beasts.

They howled a challenge in response and increased their pace, kicking up grass and dirt. At the last second, they leapt. All three became suspended in midair, captured by the webbing. Vainly they twisted and snarled but couldn't move.

The woman stared at the scene in disbelief. "How did you do that without a brush or paint?" she asked as she unlocked the cage she'd drawn. She stepped out of it, and then approached Doodles cautiously. She looked to be in her mid-thirties. She dusted off her overalls and wiped dirt from her forehead. Whatever she had just been through must have been quite a chase. There were scratches all along her arms and dirt covered her entire outfit. She brushed back her dirty blonde hair to reveal a narrow and angular face.

"I don't know how or why, but I can create things with just my hands. My name's Doodles," he said, holding out his hand.

The woman shook his hand. "Rita. Pleasure to meet you. I would have been a goner if it wasn't for you. I was headed to my camp when they caught my scent. Ever since the Eraser, the animals haven't been the same. Animals and plants are being erased at a rapid pace. This used to be such a peaceful place." She sighed as if remembering another time.

Doodles looked back at the wolves to make sure they were still stuck. "You said something about a camp?"

"Yes. The Explorers Guild. We've been working to find a way to the source of the Eraser. Someone with your talents would be invaluable. I have never seen someone draw so fast and so perfectly, let alone without the use of a paintbrush or paint. I hope you are here to help."

"Take me to your camp, please. The council sent me to find the source of the Eraser and to stop it. Whatever clues or advice your camp can offer would be a good start," Doodles said.

Rita laughed. "Normally, I would think the council was getting desperate if they were sending inexperienced boys to save Inner Earth, but I have seen firsthand what you can do, Doodles. I am lucky to have found you."

They headed off together, Rita leading the way. They crested a hill, and after shielding his eyes against the glare of the yellow-green sun, Doodles made out what appeared to be a village.

"Wait for me!" a voice cried out. Doodles and Rita turned to see Boogley waddling toward them, huffing, puffing, and waving his short stubby arms. "I can't go as fast as you long-legged folks!"

Rita turned and gave Doodles a questioning look.

"He's...well, I drew him," Doodles tried to explain to Rita.

Her nose wrinkled as she looked down at Boogley.

He puffed his furry chest out in response. "Actually, we are dear friends if you must know. Next time, wait for me. "

"I didn't know you were coming," Doodles replied.

"Of course I'm coming along. I couldn't let you do this alone now, could I? Who's your friend?"

Rita gave a curt nod and then pointed to the village. "We have to get moving. Time is short. Nighttime comes quicker these days, and strange and dangerous creatures have been wandering about at night as of late."

Doodles and Boogley shared a concerned look, and hurried to follow Rita as she walked off.

As they got closer to the town, Doodles was able to see it in greater detail. His eyes opened wide with excitement. It was a wondrous place. It was almost like he was walking in the drawings of the book his aunt and uncle gave him for his birthday. There were buildings of all shapes and sizes. Each structure was built to exemplify nature in all its unique and beautiful forms. Some of them were painted as trees, their limbs extending outward with windowed hallways. In the windowsills, glowing fireflies buzzed around in lazy circles. Winding staircases wrapped around the trunk and extended fifty feet into the air.

Another house had rooms that revolved around a bright yellow globe. Doodles realized that the house represented the solar system, its planets slowly revolving around the sun in the middle. He imagined that he would get dizzy if he lived in a house like that.

Who created something like this? he wondered.

People walked about, each of them wearing unique hats symbolic of their Wizart status. They wore bright clothing, some with jewels and elaborate decorations. Despite everyone's old age, they walked with a certain confidence and nobility, their backs straight and their heads held high. Some people nodded their way, while others ignored them. Doodles laughed as a man stumbled by on ten foot tall stilts, mumbling about how bad an idea it had been to draw them. A juggler came by, as well, juggling an assortment of colored balls. He smiled at Doodles, and even managed to tip his hat in a slight bow while keeping the balls aloft.

Doodles turned to Rita. "This place is wonderful! How could anyone want to destroy it?"

Rita seemed to ignore the question. "We can't spend much time here. We have to hurry."

He wanted to protest, but he knew she was right. They had a mission to complete, and his family was counting on him. He hurried to keep up with Rita.

"Who are these people? Do they always live here?"

Rita quickened her pace and made her way down the main dirt road to the back end of town. "This is where some Wizarts choose to retire. It's here that they can practice their craft in leisure," she told him.

Doodles nodded his understanding and continued to follow. He wondered if Riddley would come here eventually. He would certainly fit in.

Doodles spotted an elderly man pouring Dissolving Ink on a portion of his front porch that was blackened and rotting. The man then grabbed his brush and a can of paint and began to repaint. Doodles looked at Rita, who in turn nodded. "Yes, even this village is being affected by the Eraser. The Eraser first spread into the rivers and lakes. Soon the animals began to drink from the waters. It took some time for the animals to perish, and by that time they had already spread it to the plants and land. The Eraser spread—there was nothing to stop it. After we get through town, my camp is only a few more miles. Keep your eyes open and be ready for anything."

Minutes after they left town, they came upon a river, its dark, black waters running fast, jagged rocks lining the sides. From the side they were standing on, it was a good sixty feet to the other side.

"Whatever you do, don't let the water touch you," Rita warned.

Doodles gulped audibly. There was a wooden bridge spanning the river, but it was broken in some places and did not look at all sturdy.

"I'm not walking across that," Doodles said obstinately. "We'll fall in. And the water—why is it black?"

"The Eraser is corrupting everything. It is a powerful spell that is designed to spread like a virus." Doodles wondered how she knew so much about the Eraser. "We have to cross. It's the only way to get to where we're going." Rita took out her brush and began to paint while Doodles watched. She seemed to know exactly what she was doing. Doodles had drawn quite a bit in his life, but he wasn't confident enough to trust his drawings to hold two peoples' weight. He had never tested anything like this before.

Boogley tapped his foot on one of the boards Rita had just drawn, testing its strength. "I'd lie if I said I wasn't scared." He leaned closer to Doodles. "My feet are designed to swim, but it doesn't mean I would enjoy falling three stories into black—possibly toxic—water." With that he began to take small steps forward, holding his stubby arms out to the side for balance.

Rita walked slowly and carefully, Doodles right behind her as she painted the bridge. "One step at a time. Wait a few seconds after the wooden boards appear before you step on them. We want to make sure they hold."

Doodles nodded and tried not to look down. This place was certainly magical and beautiful, but it was also harsh and dangerous. If he didn't pay attention, he could find himself swallowed by the churning river below. "Almost there," Doodles said to himself. All he had to do was focus on placing one foot in front of the other. This was just like the tree he had at home he used to climb into his window. Suddenly, his footing slipped and he tripped.

His face hit hard against one of the wooden boards and he instinctively grabbed hold of them. He felt a tug at his back and realized that Boogley was holding his belt in his teeth. With a tug, Boogley began to pull him away from the edge.

Doodles lay there for what seemed like an eternity, thankful for being on something solid.

"That was a close one. Are you okay?" Rita called back to him. She had already passed to the other side.

Doodles stood up on shaky legs, mouthed a thank you to Boogley, and then continued the last few yards.

Chapter Seven

CAMP

Inner Earth was unmistakably beautiful. Doodles found himself stopping at one point to look at a group of trees. He noticed that half of their leaves were a burnt sienna color, while the other half were a deep, royal blue color. Doodles, Boogley, and Rita walked up several hills with grass the color of dark emeralds, and flowers that rose up ten feet into the sky ranging from chestnut to fuchsia. Although this was all beautiful, he also saw the effects of the Eraser as Rita lead them to her camp.

Every now and again, they would come across a dead animal or a stream that ran black from the effects of the Eraser.

They had been walking for at least an hour and all this walking made Doodles thirsty and tired. They followed a stream, and even though he knew he shouldn't drink from there, the sound and view of the water made him feel even more parched.

"I'm so thirsty," Doodles said.

"Don't worry—our camp is only about ten minutes away, and we found plenty of fresh water in a hidden cave. So far it has been untouched by the Eraser because it is so high from ground level. Who knows how long that will last, though."

Doodles sighed and continued to follow her, licking his lips. He didn't know what it was about Inner Earth, but he felt he was being watched. Maybe he was becoming delusional from dehydration.

"Rita?" Doodles asked as he swatted a bug on his neck. "What is the Eraser? When did it start? Who would want to ruin such a beautiful place? The council seemed to provide more questions than answers. All they told me was that Inner Earth was in trouble and that the Eraser was destroying it."

She pointed ahead of her to a cave opening at the top of the hill. "I am not sure how much more information I can provide. We have found some clues on the cave wall but cannot figure out what they mean. They are written in some type of ancient language. We have our top people working on it. All we know so far is that they reference the Eraser. However, we're at the Explorers Guild camp now. We'll be able to discuss matters further once we are in there. I am hoping you can help look at what we found."

Doodles was too thirsty to ask any more questions. The cave was on the crest of one of the hills they just climbed. Doodles looked around and noticed two people walking around the camp holding clipboards—they scribbled notes as they studied the various cave paintings along the wall.

A small pool of water glistened in the center of the cave. It was beautiful in its own respect, but Doodles was so thirsty that he could only describe it as looking refreshing and delicious.

Rita pointed to the two others. "Over there are Lisa and Ronald. We are the only members of the Explorers Guild that stayed behind. The rest of the group gave up when we came to this dead end."

"Pleasure to meet you," Doodles said, shaking their hands.

"Doodles is here to help track down the Eraser-the magic that is destroying this land," Rita explained.

"He looks dehydrated. For heaven's sake, let the boy drink." Lisa motioned to the pool.

Doodles was waiting for an opportunity to excuse himself properly from the conversation, and he immediately knelt down by the clear cave water and drank, scooping as much water up as quickly as he could manage.

"Refreshing, isn't it? " Rita asked. She laughed.

Doodles looked up and wiped his mouth, slightly embarrassed by how sloppy that must have looked to her. "What do you mean dead end?"

Rita pointed to the cave walls. "We finally found a path of clues that we know would lead us to the source of the Eraser. This is the last place we were lead to. There has to be a secret entrance somewhere here. The paintings on the wall have to be a clue of some sort. Perhaps whoever did this discovered the secret entrance. Whatever they placed in the heart of the mountain is going to destroy Inner Earth forever."

"How long do we have?" Doodles asked.

"Days. Maybe a few weeks. It's really hard to tell. Hey Ronald! Come say hi to our guest!" Rita yelled. Then she pointed. "Who's that? Did you come here with someone else?"

Doodles looked the direction she was pointing. It was Alanso. Doodles backed away as he prepared to draw something with which to defend himself.

Rita looked worriedly to Doodles. "What is it? What's wrong?"

"I know him. Be careful." Doodles warned.

Rita took out her brush.

Alanso held up his hands as he approached slowly. "Hold on—no need to panic. I'm here to help."

"Help us? You tried to kill me!" Doodles stammered.

Rita pointed the brush at Alanso as Lisa and Ronald drew their brushes as well.

Boogley gave the most menacing snarl he could muster.

"Kill you? You are the one who started drawing first—I assumed you were going to try to kill me first. I just wanted to take a look at your coin."

Doodles thought for a second. "No, that doesn't sound right, and that doesn't answer why you are supposedly here to help us."

Alanso shrugged. "The council sent me. Trust me, I don't want to work with you any more so than you with me."

"I don't trust you," Doodles stated.

"I don't trust you either then," said Boogley.

"You don't have to trust me. We just have to fix this little mess and then I'll be out of your hair for good."

Rita looked at Doodles and then to Alanso. There was a moment of tension, and then Doodles relaxed somewhat. "How did you find us?"

Alanso laughed. "You two are easier to track than an elephant, although I must admit that the little one's tracks threw me off."

Boogley snarled again. "Who're you calling little?"

Doodles placed a reassuring hand on Boogley's head and patted him reassuringly. "Enough. Let's just get on with it."

Doodles wasn't so sure about this whole situation, but if the council really did send him, then Doodles had no choice. Maybe Alanso was telling the truth and really created the sword out of self-defense. Something about his story didn't add up though, and Doodles made a mental note to keep his eyes open for trickery.

They spread out to search the paintings on the walls, looking for anything that would give them an idea for how to proceed. Rita and the rest of the explorers were sure that this cave led to the source of the Eraser.

Doodles stayed near Rita with Boogley close behind, still unsure of Alanso's true intentions. He found himself constantly looking back over his shoulder toward Alanso. If that man tried anything, Doodles would be ready this time.

"Over here!" Alanso hollered.

He was looking at a small script along the bottom portion of the wall, drawn with blue paint. It was in a language that Doodles didn't recognize, and from the looks on everyone else's faces, he wasn't the only one.

"You can read it?" Rita asked Alanso after seeing him silently mouthing words.

"I think so," he replied. He smiled smugly at Doodles. "It's an old language, one that I studied briefly. I dabble in languages you see and—"

"We get it, Alanso. What does it say?" Doodles said impatiently, on edge as it was.

"Well, that's the thing. It's a poem of sorts, and I'm not sure poems translate directly from their language to ours. There are cultural sayings, beliefs, slang to take into account." Alanso took out his brush and Doodles nearly jumped to hold out his hands.

"Relax, kid. I'm just getting some light in here," Alanso said as he quickly drew a lantern. After it appeared, he held it up to the script on the wall to read it more clearly:

More than one it will take

At each side of the lake

Pressing hard on the stone

The price of entry one bone

Bones of anything will not do

For you need a bone of a dragon with blue hue

You cannot draw one for it is not true

Paying the price to enter is due

Alanso put down his lantern. "Well, so much for using our talents. No drawing allowed."

Doodles looked around. "The part about the lake is pretty clear."

Rita added, "And if we can find the stones to press at the same time we should be set."

Doodles frowned. "But where will we find a dragon?"

Alanso sighed dramatically, "Must I do everything around here? I have studied Inner Earth extensively, and it just so happens I have come across a dragon's lair in my travels. The lairs are usually in remote places and hard to find if you don't know where to look. Well, come on then. I'll lead the way." He started to walk off and Doodles hesitated.

"Stay alert," he whispered to Rita. "He might be up to something." She nodded.

Alanso led the group up a series of hills. His pace was fast and determined, and Doodles wondered how often he had been to Inner Earth to know it so well. From their last encounter it was clear the man was dangerous. If he threatened a kid over a Calling Coin, there was no telling what else he was capable of. Doodles still remembered how scared he had been when he stayed home from school. He had thought Alanso would crawl through his window at any moment. Doodles didn't like the fact that he seemed so calm and smug. He was up to something. Of that much, Doodles was certain. Why was the man suddenly so willing to help out? Doodles wished Riddley was here. He would know what to do in a situation like this.

They were climbing ever higher. Each hill brought them to another, and then another as they started to wind their way toward the clouds. Ronald and Lisa didn't talk much. They stayed mostly together and talked amongst themselves for the most part. Rita stayed close to Doodles and he couldn't help but notice that she had her brush out the entire time.

As they got higher, Doodles began to wonder how they would get a bone of a blue dragon even if they could find one. Everything Doodles had ever read and seen about dragons made them look fearsome and powerful. Would anything they could draw even pierce its scales?

As they walked, Doodles realized the Eraser was getting progressively worse. The grass itself was turning black now and trees were crumbling even as he watched. Some creatures lay strewn across the landscape, obviously having drunk too much of the poisonous water, their bodies bloated and contorted or even missing some of their limbs. They smelled awful, and Doodles wanted to cover his nose from the stinging, pungent smell of decay. Far down below, he could see around for miles, jagged rocks reaching upwards like hands grasping at their little group, trying to pull them down. He gulped as he realized how high they were going.

Just when Doodles stopped to peer over the edge he heard, "Whoops!" He was pushed. As the wind rushed by his body, he hoped with uncertainty that those would not be the last words he would ever hear.

He should have reacted right away. He should have created something to get out of this situation just as he had before. But in this scary moment, Doodles could only think about his parents sitting at home waiting for him. He thought about Laura and how he never got the chance to tell her how he felt. He thought about all the things in his life that he never got a chance to do.

He felt the wind rushing by him as his fall grew faster. If he created something to fall on, it would have to be something very thick and soft. Otherwise, it would have to be something to slow his fall. Anything else and he wouldn't make it from this height. He quickly drew the only thing he could think of that he could draw quickly enough—a parachute. At least that was what Doodles pictured. What came of it was more of a makeshift balloon. It did its job though, and Doodles floated down the rest of the way.

As he landed, Doodles shook with anger. Alanso had betrayed him! Of course he had. Now he could claim all the credit for saving Inner Earth and Doodles wouldn't be around to tell the truth about Alanso being the traitor. Why hadn't he refused Alanso's help?

Doodles landed on the edge of a river. The water was stagnant and as thick as mud. This probably was once filled with crystal-clear, flowing blue water, but now it was black and a smell of rotting fish stung Doodles' nostrils. When re-telling this story, Doodles would have loved to mention that he landed perfectly. The truth, however, was that he landed face first into the edge of the river. He somehow managed to take in a mouthful of the poisonous water and he was pretty sure that something slimy brushed across his cheek as he raised his head spitting out as much of the liquid as he could. Hopefully it wasn't enough to poison him.

Doodles didn't have time to clean himself off. He had to get back up the hill to help Rita and the others. He had to beat Alanso to find the dragon. Suddenly there was a loud, rumbling sound coming from behind him. Doodles spun around.

He gasped, not daring to breathe or make a sound. He had landed right next to a dragon.

Its mighty stomach heaved up and down and its snores sounded as if the mountain itself was rumbling.

Doodles could feel the air from the great dragon's nostrils, and it burned. It blew Doodles' hair back, and threatened to roll him away. He backed up slowly and then stopped as he noted the color of the beast.

Its scales were dark blue, glinting in the sunlight. Doodles was mesmerized by the magnificent creature. No drawing could compare to this. He couldn't in good consciousness hurt such a majestic living being, even if it meant saving Inner Earth.

Everyone was relying on Doodles. They were counting on him to use his talents and to be strong. But they also said to use his heart. There had to be a way around this problem that didn't require injuring the dragon and still be able to save Inner Earth. Maybe he could draw a door into the mountain just as he did with Riddley's shop. As he thought this, he knew it was a useless idea—the mountain was too thick.

Just then the dragon woke up. It roared in pain and rolled over, scratching at its mouth with its short, scaly arms. The creature's eyes opened and looked toward Doodles.

"You are a Wizart?" The dragon's voice was a deep rumble.

Doodles wanted to run, but his feet were frozen in fear. "No...at least not yet. But I can draw."

The dragon laughed, or at least it made a snorting sound that Doodles assumed was a laugh. "You fear me?"

Doodles nodded—that was all he could manage.

"As well you should." The dragon rose up suddenly, spreading its wings out wide. "Normally, I would just eat you and be done with it, but I may need your services. I also am quite fond of games. I need a diversion to keep me from the pain I am in. We will play one."

Doodles nearly passed out with fear. "What do you mean?" He still couldn't believe that he was having a conversation with a dragon.

"The game is simple—I ask you one riddle, if you answer it correctly then I won't eat you and will also grant you one favor. However, if you answer it incorrectly, then you must draw me a favor. Then again, if you choose not to play I could just eat you and be done with it."

"No! No, I will play," Doodles said quickly, waving his hands desperately.

"Very well. Name this object: do not push me around too much because you are going to want me in your pocket when the end is near." The dragon's eyes glowed with anticipation.

Doodles thought for a moment. Every second seemed like an eternity. Was the dragon referring to the end of someone's life? He had to get the question right. If he did, then he could somehow get a bone from the dragon without hurting it, and then he could ask the dragon to help him gain access to the cave.

The dragon saw Doodles struggling to come up with an answer and it smiled in anticipation, its giant, jagged teeth glinting. It nearly blinded Doodles it was so bright. The teeth were menacing and proved to add distraction to an already stressful situation.

Miraculously, the answer came to Doodles. He had no idea how a dragon would even know about this, but he remembered playing pool with his uncle and receiving almost the same advice. "It's the eight ball. You don't want it to go in a pocket until the end of the game."

The dragon roared loudly. It slammed its feet into the dirt and shook its head back and forth. "How? No one has ever answered my riddles!"

Doodles shrugged. He didn't want the dragon to be upset and wind up eating him. Was the dragon going to keep his word?

"I don't know, it just came to me. But I'll tell you what—if you keep your word and grant me a favor I will happily help you out any way I can." Doodles stood there uncertainly as the dragon considered his options.

"You have a large heart for such a small creature," the dragon finally said. "Come here, I need to ask you a favor. Ow!" The dragon shook its head fiercely and Doodles reflexively took a step back.

Doodles realized the dragon looked like it truly was in a lot of pain. "What's wrong? Are you injured?"

"My tooth. It needs to come out. It is infected from the Eraser." The dragon howled in pain again arching its back and shaking his huge head back and forth.

"Okay, okay. Hold on. I think I can help." And then a thought occurred to Doodles. He remembered reading in a book his uncle had given him when he was younger that dragon teeth were made out of bone.

Chapter Eight

DRAGON'S TOOTH

A dragon's tooth was three times the size of Doodles. The problem now was how to pull the thing out. Then there was always the concern that the dragon would be so infuriated by the pain that he would eat him. Doodles tried not to think about that.

Rope wouldn't do—the dragon would simply rip it apart. Maybe chains would work. It would have to. Doodles began to draw long, iron chains. When they appeared, he dragged one end over to the largest tree he could find and wrapped it tightly around its base. With the other end he approached the dragon slowly.

"I'm going to have to tie this around your tooth," Doodles told the dragon.

In a million years, Doodles would never have imagined that one day he would find himself talking like this to a dragon, never mind reaching into one's mouth. If only the kids in school could see how brave he was now. There's no way that Brandon would ever attempt something like this.

"Be quick about it!" the dragon warned.

Doodles hurried. The dragon's breath was foul and he could clearly see which tooth was starting to decay and rot. He wrapped the chain around the tooth as tightly as he could.

"You're going to have to do the rest on your own," Doodles said.

The dragon nodded. It gave a roar and leapt into the air. For a second, Doodles thought there was no way such a massive creature could be held by a tree, but then—snap! The dragon's tooth flew off and with it, the tree went flying up, roots and all.

The tooth fell to the ground and sank deeply into the muddy water of the lake. Luckily, it was on the edge where the water met the muddy soil. The dragon let out one last roar and flew off.

Doodles stared at the tooth and then at his hands. It seemed like one problem or puzzle after the other. He had the tooth, but now he had to figure out what was sharp enough to cut through something as strong and sharp as a dragon's tooth.

A sledgehammer probably wouldn't be able to break a piece off of the dragon's tooth. A blowtorch wouldn't do anything either. And a sword, well that would probably just break his arm after swinging it. Doodles needed a drill. But not just any drill. He remembered from science class how NASA scientists were using a diamond-tipped drill on their Mars rover because it was the strongest material available. Then again, they also didn't know about the existence of dragons.

Will diamonds be tough enough to break off a piece of the tooth? Doodles pondered to himself.

Well, there was only one way to find out.

He tried to remember what a drill looked like. He wasn't exactly the type who used tools often. His dad had always tried to teach him to be handy around the house and Doodles had always politely declined or found an excuse. Now he wished he had paid attention.

It didn't come out that bad. Doodles was sure other people would wonder what he had created, but it worked and that's all that mattered. He practiced turning it on. It seemed pretty straightforward. He didn't really have time to waste if he was to beat Alanso to the lake.

Doodles brought the drill near the tooth and placed it against its side. With a prayer for good luck, he turned it on. Sparks flew. Doodles' arms grew tired almost instantly. The drill wasn't moving forward so he pressed even harder, using all of his strength. Slowly it sank into the tooth. He was soaked in sweat already and it had only been a minute or so. He didn't know how much longer he could hold on as both his arms vibrated until the point where they felt they would break off. With one last effort he pushed forward, bracing his feet hard into the ground. Crack!

The tooth chipped slightly, but no piece fell from it. Doodles turned the drill off and dropped it onto the mud. Doodles would have to drill another time from a different angle. He was drenched in sweat, exhausted, and scared. This was turning out to be a long day.

Doodles had been at the tooth for a good half-hour already. He was about ready to give up when a sizeable chunk finally flew off. He watched in despair as it shot out over the middle of the corrupted lake and sank. Just when he thought his luck was changing by falling right next to the blue dragon, this had to happen. There was no way he could swim into the water. Rita had warned him about it, but from the looks of it, he didn't even need that warning. It was dark and tar-like. The river smelled like decaying mold and besides that it was toxic. If even a dragon could be affected by the river, Doodles stood no chance.

He sat down, placed his head into his hands, and then cried in frustration. He had come all this way, only to fail. Inner Earth would be gone forever, his family would be disappointed in him, not to mention Riddley, and the council would never accept him as a real Wizart.

"Why are you crying?" a familiar voice sounded from behind him.

Doodles spun around to see the blue dragon back again, its wings folded up, eyeing him curiously.

"I was flying about the area and noticed you had not left. You piqued my curiosity little creature. What are you up to?"

"I lost the piece of tooth I worked so hard to get," Doodles said, this time not really caring that he was so close to such a powerful beast.

"Why do you need my tooth so badly?" the dragon asked with amusement.

"To get to the source of the Eraser, a bone from your kind is required. I lost it in the lake."

The dragon laughed, "You little creatures are strange. If you are trying to get rid of this foul Eraser, you could have just asked me."

Doodles lifted his head. "Will you help me take your tooth up to a cave on top of the hill?" He pointed. "There is a lake there that I must bring it to. It will help us stop the Eraser. I promise."

The dragon unfurled its wings and nodded. "Climb on and hold on tight. I have only ever lost four riders."

Doodles gulped. "I really wish you'd kept that last part to yourself." Just as Doodles was about to hop on, he noticed a tiny piece of the dragon's tooth on the ground, sparkling white against the mud. He bent down to pick it up. Maybe it would come in handy. It was too late to tell the dragon to forget the tooth and its offer of aid. Doodles did not want to test his luck by refusing a dragon's help. Besides, it was a long way back to the cave, and every second counted.

The dragon knelt down and Doodles climbed up its scales with uncertainty. The dragon flew faster than Doodles was comfortable with, not that riding a dragon slowly would've made him feel any more comfortable. The dragon gripped the tooth in its claws. The whole situation was surreal. Its scales were hard, shiny, and glinted brilliantly from the sunlight. He pointed northeast toward where he remembered the lake being, and the dragon followed his direction. Doodles was tempted to have the dragon make an unexpected stop next to Alanso, but the mission was too important to be wasting time confronting him now. There would be time for that later. He imagined what the look would be on Alanso's face if he came riding toward him on the back of a dragon.

"Over there!" Doodles yelled, hoping the dragon could hear him over the sound of wings beating and the wind. The dragon did, as Doodles had to hold on for dear life as the dragon dove downward, tucking his wings in close like a missile barreling down on its target. At the last second, the wings expanded and they hovered above the entrance to the cave where Rita had lead him to with the riddle painted on the walls. The lake he had drank from before seemed even more inviting than it had in the past. If he didn't have a dragon waiting impatiently for him, he may have considered taking a long drink.

Doodles didn't wait for an invitation and hopped off of the giant creature's back. He was so thankful to be on solid ground.

"Thank you," Doodles remembered to say. His Aunt Martha would be proud of him for showing good manners.

"Lead the way little one."

Doodles turned toward the cave's lake and stood straight and confident as he walked. After all, he had a dragon at his back.

The area was empty and Doodles was disappointed. He was almost looking forward to seeing Alanso here. With a dragon as his friend, Alanso wouldn't stand a chance. Doodles hoped that Rita and the rest were okay.

Doodles explained to the dragon what they were looking for, some type of stones that were different than the others. He wasn't much help. The cave was large and he didn't exactly know what he was looking for.

The dragon's keen eyesight picked out the stones after only a few minutes. They were larger than others in the cave and had a slightly bluish tint to them.

Doodles pressed on one of the stones and nothing happened. When the dragon pressed on the other stone it seemed like the entire mountain groaned in protest. There was a grinding sound as if something was moving or opening that hadn't been opened in a long, long time.

Part of the wall of the cave moved aside to reveal a long corridor made out of stone. It was dark and ominous, and Doodles felt as if they were about to trespass into something that was ancient and not meant to be disturbed.

"The entrance is too small for me, little one. You will have to continue on your own," the dragon said. After a few seconds it added, "If you do cure this foul Eraser, you will always have a friend in me. I wish you good luck little one, as I am sure you will need it."

Doodles watched the dragon leave. That was okay as he was used to being on his own. Only this time, he was more confident and he knew that he had people relying on him. No chickening out or running this time. He took a deep breath and slowly stepped over the threshold of the mountain's center at the heart of Inner Earth.

He held a lantern in his right hand as he walked. He had drawn it as soon as he entered. The wall had closed behind him as soon as he stepped through, leaving him in the pitch black. He felt claustrophobic to be in a sealed corridor in the middle of a mountain. It was still dark, despite the light of the lantern, as if the darkness wanted to swallow everything.

Doodles had been wrong in thinking that the secret opening hadn't been opened in a long time. The path had been disturbed recently. There were clear signs of that. In fact, it was hard not to see the dusty footprints on the floor. Whoever had been here did not think anyone would follow them or didn't care.

He tried to hurry as he knew time was important. His footprints sounded loud in the stone corridor. Whoosh! A net suddenly shot sideways from the wall, tangling Doodles in it. Before he could attempt to draw something to free himself, he felt his wrists being tied.

"Alanso, is that you?" Doodles called out. "You'll never get away with this!" He struggled to free his hands.

A soft voice sounded from behind him. "You think Alanso did this to you?"

Doodles struggled to turn around to see his captor. Although he recognized that voice, he was still in shock and just couldn't match a face to the voice. Whoever it was laughed. It was a cruel sounding laugh.

"When I first saw you, it was so easy to play the damsel in distress. You were so quick to jump to my rescue. And your hatred for Alanso made it so easy to stay close to you. Who'd blame me for accidently pushing you over the edge?" The voice laughed again.

"Rita?" Doodles couldn't believe it. "But why?"

Rita walked in front of Doodles' field of vision. She looked different, her face more serious and darker than he remembered. "It's nothing personal against you. I knew the council sent you. I also knew that you were their last and best hope." She caressed his face gently and he pulled back.

"Such a pity. You're so talented." She rubbed her chin thoughtfully. "Now, what to do with you...?"

"You don't have to do this! There's still time to let me go and help stop the Eraser!" Doodles was starting to panic.

"Don't you get it? I'm the one who started the Eraser. I'm the one who was rejected by the council because of their inability to change their ways! They are to blame and so this world that they value so much will be destroyed."

Doodles looked around for anything that would help him. There was nothing but the dark corridor and Rita. "Rita, think of all the beautiful creatures and land you are destroying. Is it really worth it? Can't you just talk to them?"

She shook her head. "I already tried that. They won't listen to reason. They banned me from Inner Earth in their arrogance." Rita snickered softly and mumbled to herself, "They thought banning me would keep me out. Fools!"

"Why did they kick you out of Inner Earth?"

"They are so caught up in their old, outdated ways. They wouldn't listen to the changes I had in mind. Why do we have to keep our magic secret from the world? Why not go forth and use it as we see fit? We should be the ones ruling the world! Who would stop us?"

She stepped really close to Doodles and spoke firmly and quietly. "No one is going to stop me from destroying Inner Earth. No one is going to come rescue you. No one will hear you scream."

Doodles couldn't look away from the intensity in her eyes. A shiver ran down his spine.

"I think I know what to do with you." She smiled sinisterly. "I'm going to leave you here. I want you to think about all the lies the council told you. I want you to be here when Inner Earth crumbles from within." Rita smiled at Doodles. "Yes, soon the council will realize the error of their ways."

Doodles didn't even bother struggling anymore. He knew the grip was too tight on his wrist.

She stood there as if thinking and then walked off down the corridor silently.

Doodles was left alone.

Seconds turned to minutes and minutes turned to hours. Doodles' arms were starting to fall asleep and he was both hungry and thirsty. This is not the way he thought things would go. This whole adventure had been a roller coaster of emotions and events. One minute he was flying on the back of a giant dragon, the next tied up in the center of a mountain.

Doodles wiggled his entire body, knowing it would do no good—it was more out of frustration than anything else. It wasn't fair! He had come so close. After wiggling, Doodles suddenly realized there was something in his pocket he hadn't noticed before. He didn't remember bringing anything with him. Then a thought occurred to him. When his family said goodbye, maybe one of them put something in his pocket. He wiggled again. With all the excitement of the journey, he hadn't noticed it before. Whatever it was, with all his squirming it had shifted. Doodles wiggled again, and again, until a small glowing blue coin fell out onto the floor. It was a calling coin!

Pop! Riddley appeared. "I figured you'd have used it sooner. We've all been worried sick. Why are you hanging around in a net like that wasting precious time? Aren't you supposed to be saving Inner Earth?"

Doodles laughed harder than he had ever laughed before.

Riddley and Doodles hurried down the corridor. It took almost ten minutes to catch Riddley up on current events and Rita already had a huge head start.

"When we get there, I will distract Rita. Your job is to stop the source of the Eraser. Do you understand?" Riddley sounded more serious than he had ever been. He leaned in so close to Doodles that his face was only an inch or so away. "I'm serious, Doodles. This isn't just some test."

"Yes, I know that. Just be careful. She's not as innocent as she seems." Doodles thought back to when he first rescued her from the wolves. He had thought she was weak and helpless.

Riddley nodded. "I know who she is. I was the one that banned her from Inner Earth. I convinced the council. I knew her heart was evil from the start. I should have known it was her."

They continued in silence until they saw a light ahead. The corridor became narrower, and they were forced to continue on in single file. They soon noticed an entrance into a small chamber where lava flowed from the ceiling into a large pit. As they entered the chamber, they saw that the center of the pit contained a platform with a pedestal—and that pedestal held a crystal globe. Blue light flowed freely from its base, beautifully encased in wisps of smoke, its tendrils swirling and spreading towards the edge of the cliff, and then into the molten lava below.

"That's it." Riddley pointed. "The globe. That has to be the source of the Eraser."

Rita's back was turned toward them as she watched the flow of the lava, lost in her own twisted thoughts.

"Careful now," Riddley warned. "Hide yourself while I distract her. We may only get one shot at this."

Doodles drew some lines in the air as he moved further to the side. If this was to work, he had to be out of Rita's line of sight. He drew a pile of rocks and ducked behind them. There were other piles of rocks strewn about and Doodles just hoped that he would not look too out of the ordinary.

Riddley called out, "Rita, I have come to stop you!"

She turned around quickly, her brush already out and ran toward Riddley without hesitating. Doodles wanted to watch and see what happened, but he couldn't afford the luxury.

He jumped over the pile of rocks and dashed toward the globe. He heard sword fighting from behind him. Whatever was happening, Riddley was doing his share, counting on Rita's over-confidence and anger to cloud her judgment. Just as Doodles was about to grab onto the globe he heard a cry for help. It was Riddley's voice. Doodles hesitated for a second, but then attempted to knock the globe into the lava. It didn't budge. He braced his feet firmly and pushed again with all of his strength, straining his legs and arms as much as possible. Nothing moved, not even an inch. He drew the chip of dragon's tooth from his pocket and jammed it as hard as he could into the globe. It shattered into thousands of tiny, crystal pieces. One last puff of putrid smoke billowed out—and then there was silence. Doodles turned around just in time to see Riddley and Rita falling over the edge toward the lava below.

Doodles noticed in horror that both Riddley's and Rita's paintbrushes were left up on the ledge. Without their brushes, they would plummet into the lava. He felt sick to his stomach. He had ignored Riddley's call for help in order to destroy the globe. *He could have saved him. He could have at least tried!*

Then a thought occurred to Doodles, and he realized what he could do. He hoped it wouldn't be too late. He started to draw as quickly as he could. The heat from the lava and a sudden feeling of exhaustion being so far underground were almost unbearable. Doodles gritted his teeth and ignored the sweat pouring down his forehead. It seemed like an eternity before the drawing was complete.

Doodles waited impatiently. Nothing happened. He was too late. Riddley had sacrificed himself to save Inner Earth. Doodles' eyes began to tear up. The old man was eccentric, but he was one of the best friends he'd ever had. He would miss him.

"I know I told you to never draw me again, but in this case I'm happy you broke the rules."

Doodles looked up. "Riddley!"

Chapter Nine

BACK TO SCHOOL

It was strange going back to school after everything he'd been through. Everyone treated Doodles the same at first, thinking he'd still been home sick. But soon they realized that something about him was different. He had grown confident seemingly overnight. Doodles walked with his head held high. He looked everyone in the eyes and spoke with more confidence. Even Brandon steered clear after Doodles stood up to him. Doodles learned that Brandon's father had recently left the house. Doodles felt bad for Brandon in a way, and now understood where Brandon's anger came from. Doodles' family no longer pressured him to do things he didn't really want to do, although his father did make the occasional reference to basketball tryouts.

Boogley had waited for Doodles loyally after he was pushed off the cliff. His parents even allowed Boogley to sleep in his room, although Doodles was starting to regret that decision. Boogley talked non-stop during the night, and apparently didn't need any sleep.

There had been a celebration the day after Doodles had returned home. Rita had fallen into the lava and Alanso was missing. They would never bother Inner Earth or Wizarts again. The world seemed a lot safer to Doodles. Even the council members had shown up to the celebration, still wearing their usual dark robes and overly elaborate hats. Council member Brian still gave his usual scornful look, but there was a hint of a smile at the corner of his eyes. There was ice cream, cake, and a cookout. They did things the old fashioned way, without use of drawing magic. People took turns patting Doodles on the back or giving him words of appreciation. Some of the Wizarts from the conference in England had made it back just in time for the celebration. Doodles felt like he was floating on a cloud. Inner Earth had been saved, he had made his family proud, and he had learned so much about himself and what he was capable of.

Even Riddley attended, although he bothered most of the guests with his elaborate stories.

At the celebration, he remembered Uncle Roger winking at him from across the yard as he manned the grill. Doodles remembered wondering how any food was left over after his uncle cooked.

When the celebration was nearing its end, Riddley approached Doodles. "Your second quest begins tomorrow. Remember, it takes three quests to become a full Wizart." Riddley waved three fingers in front of Doodles' face for emphasis.

Doodles laughed. "Even after I saved Inner Earth?"

Riddley shrugged. "Rules are rules. I assume you have been studying?"

Doodles rubbed his eyes and grinned. It hadn't even been but a few days since he saved Inner Earth. "Don't you have customers to tend to?"

Riddley smiled. "There are always customers. Off with you then."

"Riddley, this is my house."

"Oh, well, then off I go. See you tomorrow for the next quest." Riddley grabbed one more hot dog on the way out.

Doodles watched him leave. What a strange old man. As Doodles enjoyed his moment of victory, deep within Inner Earth, a hand grabbed onto a ledge.

Slowly, and with great effort, Rita pulled herself up. She picked up her paintbrush and didn't even bother to dust herself off. She was covered in dust and ashes from head to toe.

Her clothes had been ripped in many places from the jagged rocks that covered the side of the wall.

She plucked a single bristle off of her brush and let it fall into the waiting depths of the flowing lava. Her eyes were determined and locked onto the deadly lava below her. Her grip on the brush tightened until her fingers turned white.

"This isn't over. I'm coming for you, Doodles."

The End

About Russell D. Bernstein

ussell David Bernstein was born in Miami, FL. He currently resides in Orange, CT where he actively pursues his writing career. He takes writing and acting classes at the Actors Gym in Hamden, CT. He has a passion for the arts and continually engages in refining his acting and writing ability on a daily basis.

Russell's background in working with children, specifically those with troubled pasts, inspired him to write a book on the topic of overcoming bullying and the power of creativity. His book is meant to inspire, entertain, and open the reader's minds to the concept that creativity and perseverance—rather than just strength and athleticism—can be a strong asset.

CPSIA information can be obtained at www.ICGtesting.com
Printed in the USA
BVOW03s1341091014

370111BV00005B/9/P